DOYLES
CASEBOOK
REVISITED

By

ANN BRADY

Copyright Written Work: © Ann Brady 2021
Copyright Images: © Ann Brady 2021

Publisher: Pen & Ink Designs 2021

ISBN: 9780993112928

CONTENTS

Other Works by the Author

Fiction:

Dear Friends: Letters From Abroad – Historical Fiction
Doyle's Casebook – Edition 1 – Crime Fiction
Little Friends – Picture Books
      Woodland Adventures Series x 6 books
      Garden Adventures Series x 6 books
      Farmyard Adventures Series x 6 books
Little Friends Colouring Book

Dracula: The Untold Story – Mystery/Horror Fiction
  (co-written with Rex Greenwood, decd)

WHO IS TOMMY DOYLE

Tommy Doyle is an ex-Detective Inspector in his mid-forties. He lives alone in an old three-story, brownstone building, in a district of LA. Tommy joined the police force after leaving school, much the same as his father and grandfather had before him.

During his time in the force, he met, fell in love with, and married a sweet girl called Mary. Much to both their regrets, they never had children, and as such Mary found the loneliness and stress of being a policeman's wife unbearable. There were many nights when Tommy didn't come home with Mary not knowing if he was alive or not. Doyle mixing with an assortment of bad guys often frightened her so in time, she came to hate his job.

The final straw for Mary came when Doyle's partner, Pete Mackintosh, came close to being shot dead. Fortunately, Doyle had turned the corner at just the right moment, saving his partner from some mad nutter who thought it would be fun to shoot a cop. The incident created a strong bond of friendship between the two men, which still existed to this day.

But for Mary, it was the end; she couldn't take it anymore.

Telling Tommy, they had drifted apart she made him choose - her or his job. It was a hard decision for Tommy; but even so, Mary wasn't surprised when he actually chose the job. Fortunately, they parted amicably. Mary eventually married a grocer and lives somewhere upstate. They also have three children, so she is happy, and for Doyle, that is all that matters.

After Mary left, she would often ring him, checking up to see how he was doing. As time passed the calls slowly petered out. It had been nearly ten years now since they had seen or spoken to each other. If truth be known Tommy did occasionally Miss Mary. It had been nice to come home to a warm house and a cooked meal. 'Oh well,' he had thought, 'it's all water under the bridge.'

Having left the force over three years ago; disillusioned and disappointed, Tommy had become a PI - setting up Doyle's Investigations. He had been a police officer for close to twenty years but had been driven out. Like Tommy and his pal Mac, most of his fellow officers believed he had been set up, but they couldn't confirm that.

It had happened whilst Tommy was working undercover.

Six months into the job he had discovered someone was trying to involve him in a criminal setup. Following twelve months of being investigated Tommy had been hauled before a disciplinary committee. He'd only just managed to avoid being incriminated when a surprise witness had come forward and exonerated him. Still, the whole experience had left a very sour taste in his mouth.

Fortunately, both he and the other officers at the precinct knew a local con-man had been involved, although the guy had somehow managed to avoid capture. Perhaps he had been forewarned and had fled the state, leaving Doyle's fellow officers with suspicions that someone within the force was behind the whole affair. Unfortunately, it was something they couldn't prove or follow up on, as connections with those 'upstairs,' meant the guy was protected.

About four months after being cleared Doyle made the decision to retire, or maybe he'd resigned due to being let down by those upstairs? It all depended on your point of view. Being disillusioned, and with the lack of support from senior management, it seemed it wasn't what you knew, but more a question of who you knew. He also found he didn't like the politics of the modern police force.

'I know who you are,' thought Doyle as he walked away from the precinct. 'And one day, you will pay. One day, wherever you are, I will get revenge.' Not that Doyle was one to bear grudges, but he never forgot where a debt was owed; either by him or to him.

As it turned out leaving the police force worked out quite well for Tommy. He'd set up his office on the first floor of the old brownstone building he called home. He had used his savings to rent two ground-floor rooms, setting up a spare bedroom in one room alongside his office. Eighteen months later a relative had passed away, leaving him with a sizeable inheritance. It meant he didn't have to work if he chose not to. When the owner of the building also passed away the brownstone came up for sale so Tommy put an offer in and purchased it. Overnight, he went from tenant to landlord.

Using some of the inheritance he moved his office upstairs to the second floor, converting the top floor into an apartment for himself. There was enough room to have a large sitting room, kitchen, and two bedrooms with ensuite bathrooms. At first, the ground floor rooms were made into 2 apartments, which he rented out to reputable people. But, more often than not he left them empty. After all, he didn't need the money.

Being a PI can sometimes be dangerous, so after much consideration Doyle decided to adapt the building, making it more secure. Once the last tenants had left, he'd had a small brick extension built at the back of the brownstone. To ensure secrecy he had used the services of a builder from out of town. The extension contained a hidden staircase that ran from the top floor to the bottom. To complete the job, a secret door leading to the staircase in the extension was installed in a store cupboard in his office. By the time the staircase was finished anyone visiting would be unaware of the buildings' secret. The idea of this secret entrance/exit would give him an alternate escape route, should he ever need one? So far, he hadn't needed one, but you never knew what might happen.

With Doyle's office now being on the second floor, he decided to expand the size of it. He added a kitchen and a bathroom, with extra rooms for storage and a gym.

Eventually, he converted the two ground-floor apartments into office units, which he rented out. The idea being, that as offices usually closed around five pm, he would have the whole building to himself in the evenings. It proved to work out well for him.

Over the last three years, Tommy had enjoyed being a PI. He still had links to the police force through his good friend Mac who occasionally helped him out with some bits of information; all unbeknown to the new man in charge, one Lieutenant Johnstone. Mac knew Johnstone disliked Tommy, but still, it didn't stop him from helping his mate when necessary. Mind you he wasn't the only one, as his colleagues were not averse to Dropping the odd helpful bit of information when Tommy needed it; as long as the Lieutenant wasn't looking.

Regardless of missing working on the Police force, and being around the guys he'd known for so many years, Tommy had slowly built up quite a solid reputation within his local community.

His favourite place to eat and hang out was O'Malley's Bar & Diner. A middle-aged Irish couple ran the bar; Pat O'Malley and his wife Molly, who cooked the food. She made a 'mean' Stew & Dumplings, Tommy's favourite.

The fact Doyle was an ex-copper wasn't held against him, and it had probably helped, as his presence had made the community feel much safer knowing he lived close by.

The following short stories are based on some of Tommy's cases.

WHODUNIT!

The street was quiet and deserted. Nothing stirred; not a dog, cat, or any other human being. Only the fluttering of the leaves and swishing of the bushes moved, stirred by the cool breeze gently blowing along the street. Up above the street light flickered. The watcher turned up the collar of his raincoat, whilst moving further back into the shop doorway. Tommy Doyle had been standing in that doorway for quite some time.

Looking at his watch Tommy realised it had been over an hour since the man in the house opposite had turned the corner at the top of the street. He had watched as the man had walked towards the house, head down but still aware of his surroundings.

Reaching the gate of the house nearest the flickering street lamp, the man had stopped. Taking a packet out of his pocket he had put a cigarette in his mouth, before returning the pack to his pocket. Cupping his hands around a lighter to light the cigarette, he had taken a few deep puffs, until the tip of the white tube glowed red. All the while he had surreptitiously looked up and down the street.

Satisfied he hadn't been followed the man had turned, opened the garden gate, and walked to the door, still constantly checking the coast was clear. Three sharp raps had followed and within seconds the door had opened. He had quickly passed through, not speaking a word.

Doyle settled down to wait.

Lighting a cigarette of his own Doyle began wondering what the hell he was doing waiting here. Annoyingly, it seemed these days wayward husbands and wives were his 'bread and potatoes.' He sighed, what he wouldn't give for a good solid job with some adventure in it, instead of standing in cold draughty streets waiting to catch evidence of someone's infidelity. He sighed again.

Forty minutes later the house door opened and the man came out. Turning, he quietly said goodbye to the lady who remained hidden inside. Doyle knew what she looked like as he had waited once to follow her. He moved as far back into the doorway as possible, not wanting to be seen. The man opposite looked around and satisfied the street was deserted, he quickly left, setting off up the street at a steady pace.

As soon as the door closed Doyle left his hiding place, and followed the man at a safe distance, keeping him in sight. Doyle walked with his head down, giving the impression that he just happened to be there. Having nothing to do with the man in front. Not that it mattered as the man didn't look back; he just kept on walking, a small smile flitting across his face. He was feeling happy.

Fifteen minutes later the man turned the corner towards the house where he lived. Doyle not far behind turned the corner then stopped. Looking up the street he noted a lot of activity; blue flashing lights with people milling around. The man stopped, then suddenly started running towards the commotion.

Nearing his house, he slowed as someone suddenly stepped out, asking him who he was. Doyle overheard him breathlessly explaining it was his house, as he wanted to know what had happened. The person stepped back into the light of the nearest car and Doyle saw it was a police officer.

'Oh, Oh,' thought Doyle, 'what's going on here?' After the man had entered the house, he headed straight towards the officer, whom he had recognised.

"Whoa there, Smithy," Doyle called out, "how are you doing bud?"

The office looked up and seeing Doyle sauntered over to him. "Not bad Tommy and you?"

"Fine, just fine," replied Doyle, "So, what's going on here then?"

Looking around, Officer Smith, bent his head towards Doyle, saying breathlessly, "Murder! Looks like the lady of the house disturbed a burglar and came off the worse for it. It's pretty messy in there," whereupon the officer shuddered. Despite his years on the force the young man could still not get used to finding a bloody mess; especially when the victim was a good-looking woman.

"Who's in charge, Smithy?" asked Doyle.

The office looked around again before answering, "Johnstone."

'Hell,' thought Doyle, the last person he wanted to see. There was bad history between the two men from when Doyle had been on the force. Doyle had got the upper hand and Johnstone had never forgiven him.

'Oh well,' he thought, 'better leave it for tonight.' Quickly saying goodnight, he left the scene. He could get all the information he needed later from other sources.

* * * *

The following morning Doyle strolled into the local precinct. As usual, he was greeted with jokes and banter; all light-hearted, as most of the guys knew and liked Tommy. To them, he was solid, straightforward, with many remembering the incident resulting in Doyle's early retirement. Feeling he'd been badly treated they usually did their best to assist him whenever they could.

"Hey there, Doyle," shouted one of the officers from across the room, "To what do we owe this honour?"

Doyle looked towards the speaker, and seeing his mate Mac, DI Pete Mackintosh, he smiled. Going towards him he held his hand out in greeting, saying, "Mac, how you doing pal?"

"Fine, just fine," responded Mac standing up. At over six feet tall with red hair Mac showed his Scottish heritage by the lilt in his voice. The pair shook hands warmly as he offered Doyle a cup of coffee, which was gratefully accepted as he hadn't eaten breakfast.

The pair bantered words until Mac asked, "So Tommy what do you want? A case you need help with? Tell me before Johnstone arrives and sees you. He wasn't too pleased to know you were hanging around the murder scene last night. By the way, what were you doing there?"

Doyle looked up in surprise he hadn't seen the Lieutenant but somehow the man must have seen him. 'Damn,' thought Doyle, before answering, "I was following the guy who lives there."

At this response, Mac's head shot up in surprise; a questioning look on his face. "The wife employed me to follow her old man. I've been on him for about three weeks. He's been having an affair with a very pretty blonde called Gloria," Doyle explained.

Mac whistled, "Wow. Johnstone thinks it was a burglary gone wrong but this could put a different slant on the whole affair."

Doyle, shaking his head said, "You mean maybe the husband did it. No way. I'm his alibi, so how…?" Suddenly Doyle was cut off mid-stream.

"Doyle. What the hell are you doing here," yelled a voice, trying to sound tough, which wasn't easy as the voice was too effeminate. Both Mac and Doyle looked up to see Lieutenant Johnstone stalking towards them.

"Who the hell let you in?" snarled Johnstone. "Get lost."

Doyle stretched himself up to his full six feet four-inch height, meaning he overshadowed the

Lieutenant in what could be construed a menacing way. Johnstone stepped back. Secretly he was afraid of Doyle but there was no way he would show it in front of his fellow officers. He knew Doyle was well-liked but he hated the sight of the man, doing all he could to prevent him from visiting the precinct.

Although Doyle reciprocated Johnstone's feelings, he wouldn't let it show so, in an amiable voice, he said, "Hi Johnstone, how you doing?" Then sounding full of innocence, he asked, "Any progress on last night's murder?"

The Lieutenant fumed, responding, "It's in hand Doyle, and nothing to do with you so get out of here before I have you thrown out," and turning he headed for his office.

"Oh," said Doyle in a loud voice, "then you won't want any information regarding the case then?"

Johnstone stopped, fuming he turned, sarcastically asking, "And why exactly do you think I would be interested in any information you could possibly give me about a case."

Doyle shrugged. Turning he walked towards the doorway, calling out, "If that's the case then you won't want to know where the husband was last night?" And with that he passed through the office doors waving bye to his mates, a big grin spread across his face.

Johnstone watched him leave, before turning on Mac demanding to know what Doyle had meant. Mac shrugged his shoulders, telling the Lieutenant he hadn't got a clue as Tommy had only just arrived.

Johnstone raged inside. He couldn't let Doyle go without hearing what he had to say. If he didn't find out then his men would say he wasn't doing his job right.

'Damn the man,' he thought, before telling Mac, "Get him back in here. I want to know what he knows."

Slowly Mac left the room grinning, catching up with Doyle just he was getting into his car. Hailing Tommy, he said, "Johnstone wants you back inside. Wants to know what you know."

Doyle smiled. "Tell him you missed me. He's a moron and doesn't deserve my time of the day. I'll call back later; something I need to check out first," and with that, he fired up his car and drove away.

Returning to the squad room Mac passed on the news of having missed Doyle. Johnstone wasn't happy, knowing he could do nothing until Doyle returned. In the meantime, he would have the husband brought in and questioned. Maybe he could get one up on Tommy Doyle.

Driving along Tommy thought about the previous evenings' events. It seemed a little too convenient that the husband had been elsewhere the moment his wife was killed. Maybe it was just coincidence but too many years on the force dealing with scum bags had honed Doyle's mind into thinking the worse. 'I'm becoming cynical,' he thought, sighing deeply.

The first place Doyle went was to the crime scene. He was just in time to witness the husband being taken away in a police car. No doubt he had got Johnstone thinking. Laughing to himself he left the car and approached the house. Fortunately, he knew the officer standing guard, grateful that he turned a blind eye whilst Tommy entered the house. Once inside he looked around. The wife's bedroom, the scene of the murder, had been cordoned off. Bending under the tape across the doorway Tommy entered the room.

Looking around he realised this was definitely a woman's room; very feminine in both design and decor. Checking the cupboards and wardrobes, he saw no sign of the husband; none of his clothes or personal effects. There was little else to see. Leaving the room, he wandered along the landing. Entering another bedroom, he discovered the husband's things laid out. Quickly searching drawers and wardrobes he found nothing. Satisfied he wouldn't discover anything of interest Doyle left the house, spending a few minutes chatting to the officer before climbing into his car and driving off.

Doyle's next visit was to the house of the woman the husband had been seeing. He knocked at the door and waited. No one was in. Looking around to ensure he wasn't being watched Doyle slipped around the back of the house. Fortunately, the back door was shielded by the trees in the garden. There was no alarm, so taking out his lock pick Tommy unlocked the back door. Hearing the click of the lock he gently turned the handle and, after checking once more he wasn't being watched, he quickly slipped inside.

The place was reasonably tidy, although the breakfast pots were still in the sink. She had left in a hurry; perhaps late for work. Quickly and quietly, Doyle went through the downstairs of the house searching each room carefully, looking for anything to help him uncover the truth about the relationship.

Finally, he mounted the stairs. Passing the bathroom, he noted men's toiletries sat on a shelf alongside the usual women's stuff. Opening the next door, he noted a small single bed, sewing machine but little else. Quickly closing the door, he moved on to the next room. It was the master bedroom. There was a nightdress lying across a neatly made bed. On the dresser, more signs of a woman's presence, hairbrush, make-up, and perfume. A laddered stocking had been half dropped into a waste bin. Doyle ignored it.

Crossing to the wardrobe he checked the contents; there was nothing of interest. Closing the doors, he returned to the dressing table and began searching the drawers. The top drawer held an assortment of underwear in different colours and a variety of stockings. The second drawer held other lingerie. Doyle moved it about looking under the items. Women were known to hide things, but there was nothing. Finally, he pulled at the bottom drawer. It wouldn't open. He pulled harder. It was locked.

'Interesting,' he thought, now why would she keep this drawer locked. Bending down he took out his door picks, easily unlocking the drawer. Inside were a bunch of letters and a buff file. Taking them out Doyle sat on the bed, spreading the papers across the cover. The letters were addressed to the owner of the house.

Opening the buff file, he began checking the contents. On top was a report. Reading it Tommy was surprised by its contents. Having quickly read the report he whistled loudly; shocking even himself by the sound of the noise. Underneath the report was a packet. Picking it up, he opened it and withdrew a bundle of photographs. Looking at the images Doyle's face changed colour.

'My God,' he thought, 'what the hell am I going to do now?'

He knew he couldn't take the items as they'd be missed; besides, breaking and entering would give Johnstone the ideal reason to throw him in jail. Taking out the small camera he always carried he spread the photos on the bed and promptly began snapping. Finally, he photographed the report. Quickly returning everything to the buff file, he placed it back in the drawer, locking it securely.

Having finished his perusal of the room, Doyle ensured everything was as it had been when he entered. He was fortunate he had a good memory, being able to memorise a room in seconds, thus ensuring nothing was out of situ' when he left. Satisfied he left the room ready to descend the stairs.

The sudden noise of a key being placed in the front door made Tommy stop in his tracks. Quickly he returned to the empty room. Waiting, he swore under his breath as he listened to the voices below. It was the woman with the murdered woman's husband.

"What do you mean everything will be okay," demanded the male voice.

The woman responded softly, her voice cloying at the man's senses, "I told you darling there is nothing to worry about. Everything will be okay."

"No, it's not," shouted the man. "For God's sake, I got arrested. They even accused me of killing my wife."

"Did you tell them where you were when it happened?" asked the woman.

"I told them I was out walking, but I don't think they believed me. What the hell am I to do? I didn't kill her but how do I prove it?" the man whined.

The rest of the conversation was lost on Doyle as he quietly sneaked down the stairs and let himself out of the house. Fortunately, the couple were too wrapped up in themselves to notice him disappearing down the garden path.

Returning to his car Doyle took out his camera to look at the photos he had taken. 'Hmm,' he thought, 'what a turn up for the books.' The question was, what was Doyle going to do with them. These could make a big difference to the investigation. 'The problem will be Johnstone; he's not going to listen to anything I tell him,' thought Doyle. 'At least not without trying to cause trouble for me.'

As Doyle pondered the problem the man left the house, hurrying past Doyle's car. Spotting him, Tommy left his car and followed, deciding to check where he was going.

The man disappeared around the corner. Following him, Tommy watched as the man stopped alongside a big limousine. Slowly he climbed into the back seat. Stopping Doyle made a point of searching his pockets for cigarettes, whilst watching the car slowly pull away. Trying to spot who was in the vehicle was hard as the windows were blacked out.

'Strange,' thought Doyle. 'This is getting more and more interesting.'

Once the car had pulled away Tommy quickly returned to his own car.

Catching up with the limousine, he followed at a safe distance, still trying to work out who the vehicle belonged to. Picking up his mobile he rang Mac and gave him the registration.

Within seconds, Mac asked, "What the hell have you got yourself into, Tommy? Do you know who that car belongs to?"

"If I knew I wouldn't have needed to ask," replied Doyle.

"Be careful, Tommy," his friend warned him after supplying the name. "You could get into some serious trouble."

"Yea, I know, I know. Trust me, Mac. I'm like a cat, I have nine lives. I'll get back to you shortly," and with that Doyle signed off, not hearing Mac swear out loud.

The black car had stopped up ahead, the man, having stepped from the car, was stooping to listen to the person sat inside, before turning away to hail a taxi.

'Very strange,' thought Doyle, 'perhaps it's time to discover what the hell is really going on here.'

Tommy was left with two choices; follow the man in the taxi or the car. It didn't really matter, as he had both names and addresses.

'To hell with it,' he thought, 'it's time for lunch.'

Moving away, he took the next turning and headed back to the precinct, arriving in time to catch Mac going for lunch.

Deciding on a dog and coffee from the local café, they headed for the nearby small park. There they could talk without being overheard.

Mac asked Tommy what the hell was happening.

Telling his friend all he knew, the pair eventually sat down to look through the photos on Doyle's camera.

"Hell," said Mac, "are these genuine? Where the hell did you get 'em?"

"As far as I'm aware, they're real," responded Doyle. "And, you don't want to know where I got them."

Mac looked at his pal, saying nothing, but understanding that sometimes a PI has to break the rules to obtain the information needed. Besides, what he didn't know wouldn't hurt either of them. There were enough crooks in the world so if occasionally, you had to bend the rules to catch 'em, then hey ho! Like Doyle, Mac was old school, which was why he and Tommy got on so well. They had also been partners for over eighteen years while Tommy was on the force.

"So, what are we going to do?" asked Mac.

Doyle didn't answer straight away, he was thinking more of what he could do. "Not sure, but I need to find out more before I give Johnstone the

28

info. The question is whether or not the husband set his wife's murder up? If he didn't, then who did?" responded Tommy.

"Sooner you than me, pal. But, if you need help you know where I am," said Mac and with that, he left Tommy sitting on the bench.

'Mac is right,' thought Doyle, 'I'll have to tread carefully. I need to do a bit more digging.' Finally, he decided to speak to the neighbours. They usually knew what was going on and they loved to gossip, especially the old dears. Leaving the park, he made his way to his car.

Half an hour later Doyle pulled up in the street next to the one he wanted; if the police were still around, better to not advertise his presence. All he had to do was come up with a reason for asking questions. Strolling down the street Doyle chose the house directly opposite the murder scene. Making sure he looked tidy he knocked on the door. Shortly afterward the door was opened by a lady of indeterminate age.

"Good day ma-am," said Doyle smiling, "I was wondering if you could help me?"

The woman looked queerly at him, before asking, "What do you want?"

Flashing his PI ID, he began explaining how he was trying to discover something about the incident that had happened across the road. The lady, being wary, asked if he was a reporter? Doyle quickly denied it, explaining he represented local insurance companies who were concerned about the area. He was asking all residents their opinion about safety in the neighbourhood. The woman questioned him as to which insurance company, so Doyle reeled off a few names. Relaxing, the woman quickly invited him inside.

Once indoors Tommy agreed to some refreshments, spinning out his tale about the insurers. Soon the lady opened up, giving her opinion about all 'the goings on' regarding the house across the road.

An hour later Doyle left, having learnt a great deal; in fact, much more than he expected. Returning to his office he mulled over what he had learnt; but what do with the information. He finally decided to sleep on it. Tomorrow was another day.

* * * *

The following morning, as Tommy sat in his office, there was a knock at the door. Calling 'enter' he was surprised when the husband of the murdered wife entered. Slightly shocked, he managed to greet the man as if he didn't know who he was. Formalities over Doyle asked what he could do for him.

Sitting, the man began, "Mr. Doyle I need your help. I've been accused of killing my wife."

Surprised by the confession, Tommy cleared his throat, asking, "And in what way do you think I can assist you, Mr. Err? Surely you need an attorney."

"Benson," replied the man, "Charles Benson. I already have an attorney. The problem is, I also thought I had an alibi but he doesn't believe me. The person I spent the evening with can't be found, and I don't know why. I need your help Mr. Doyle, and quickly before the police arrest me."

Doyle took a moment to digest the man's reply, before asking, "But surely you know where the person lives."

"Oh yes. I gave my attorney the details but he says the house is empty. I just don't understand it. I have been going there for the last six weeks. I don't know what is happening to me!"

Tommy studied Benson. He certainly appeared to be in emotionally dire straits but wondered if it was an act. As he watched, Tommy suddenly realised the man was genuinely distraught and possibly was telling the truth. Taking a breath, he said, "Cup of coffee, Mr. Benson. It will help calm you while you tell me everything."

Passing a mug of coffee to Benson, Tommy returned to his seat, saying, "Begin, Mr. Benson. Tell me it all, right from the beginning."

Taking a deep breath, Mr. Benson began pouring out his sorry tale; starting with how he and his wife had been going through a bad patch. He thought she had been cheating, so he had foolishly got himself embroiled with a pretty young blonde woman. As Benson finished talking, he sat back, feeling exhausted, and waited for Doyle's reaction.

Silence swirled the room while Tommy studied Benson, before responding, "Okay Mr. Benson, I presume you want me to find this young woman?"

"Do you think you can," asked Benson, sitting up eagerly?

"I can't promise, but I will certainly try," replied Doyle, "My usual terms are $50 a day, plus expenses."

Agreeing Benson pulled out his cheque book, handing over a payment of $150 for three days of Doyle's employment. Pocketing the cheque Doyle promised to contact the man as soon as he found something out.

Once Benson had left, Doyle sat thinking over the turn of events. Either the man was a good actor, or he genuinely wasn't involved in his wife's death. 'Of course,' reasoned Tommy with himself, 'he might know I have been following him, and this is all a smoke screen.' Deciding the first thing to do was check out the love nest, he left his office.

Half an hour later Doyle pulled up in front of the house. Knocking on the front door he waited. No-one answered. Going around to the back garden he used his lock pick to enter the house unseen.

The kitchen was empty of any items. Carrying on through the house he found the front room, neat but any furniture was now covered with white sheets. Upstairs the bathroom was clear of all paraphernalia; not even a toilet roll could be seen.

The first bedroom was unchanged, apart from dust sheets over the furniture. Continuing along the landing, he discovered the front bedroom was also covered with dust sheets. The wardrobe was now empty. Opening the dressing table drawers, he found the bottom one was now unlocked and empty. Whoever the woman had been she had certainly disappeared.

Going back downstairs, Doyle let himself out of the house and returned to the front garden. A gentle voice suddenly asked, "Are you buying the house?"

Turning, Doyle noted an old lady leaning on the fence. Approaching her he smiled, saying, "I didn't know it was up for sale. An old friend of mine lived here. Do you know where she's gone?"

"She left two days ago."

Putting a disappointed look on his face, Tommy said, "Oh dear. I've missed her. Don't suppose you know where she's gone do you?"

The old lady smiled, saying, "I might. Would you like a cup of tea?"

"Why not. Sounds a good idea," and Doyle jumped over the low wall between the two houses to follow her indoors.

An hour later he left, having gained more information than he had envisaged receiving. The plot was thickening, or so it seemed.

Heading back to his office, Doyle called in at the precinct. Perhaps it was time to give Mr. Benson a break. Predictably Johnstone was not overly pleased to see him.

"What do you want, Doyle?" snarled the Lieutenant.

Doyle looked at the man, hurt surprise written across his face, as he said, "I got a message you wanted to see me, Lieutenant."

"Humph," sniffed Johnstone, "well, yes. You said you had some info about the Benson murder. What is it?"

Doyle cast a glance and a sneaky wink at Mac, before responding. "Well, I thought you should know that the husband has an alibi."

Surprised, Johnstone asked, "Oh yes. And just what would you know about it?"

Doyle sighed. "Because I was tailing him. On the night of the murder, he was at the house of a blonde woman, from seven-thirty until nine pm, after which he returned home to find you there."

Johnstone waited, calming his breathing. "And where exactly is this house?"

Doyle gave him the address. Johnstone began issuing instructions to have the woman brought in, but he hadn't got far when Doyle said, "No point, the house is empty. She cleared out two days ago."

"And how would you know that?"

"Because Mr. Benson asked me to investigate her disappearance," Doyle responded smilingly.

The Lieutenant was annoyed. Hell, he thought he had got the husband for the murder. Damn, it would have done his career good to have broken the case so quickly. Doyle's alibi now spoilt everything. Now he would have to investigate further.

"Are you sure he was there," asked Johnstone?

Producing his notebook, Doyle showed his notes. Then he produced a timed photograph for the day in question clearly showing what time the husband had left the blonde, which just happened to coincide with the murder. Benson was in the clear. He could not have done the crime.

Johnstone stormed into his office, clearly very unhappy at Doyle's interference.

Mac said, "Ahhh... You've just upset him, Tommy lad. Are you sure about the man?"

Doyle turned. "The man was at the house. And with the time frame, there was no way he could have killed her as I was following him."

"Case closed on him, then?" said Mac. "Yes?"

"No," replied Doyle. "I said he didn't kill her; I didn't say he wasn't involved. That's the next thing to find out," and with that, he waved bye and left the squad room.

Leaving the precinct, Tommy began to wonder whether Benson was involved in his wife's death. The more he thought about it, the more he doubted the fact. But, how to prove it.

Two days later, Mr. Benson returned to Doyle's office, wanting to know if anything had been discovered. Tommy didn't have much to report but needed to ask the man a few personal questions about his late wife. He was expecting him to be difficult.

Doyle began, "Well, Mr. Benson, you will have heard that I've given you an alibi for the evening in question."

Benson, admitting he had been surprised by the news, asked, "Why were you following me?"

Leaning across, Tommy replied, "Your wife asked me to find out who your lady friend was. She obviously knew you were having an affair. Did you know she knew? After all, that would be the perfect excuse for murder."

Benson's eyes flew open with shock, replying adamantly, "No. I did not know my wife knew. I told you we were having some marital problems." Then sighing, he explained. "It was the other way round. My wife has had several affairs over the last few years. I've always forgiven her, as they were often short-lived, but lately, she seemed to be more withdrawn and distant. I thought maybe this time it was different. That it was serious," and he paused before concluding, "I thought that if I did the same, she might come to her senses and finish the relationship. That's why I took up with Gloria."

This was an age-old story, and one Doyle was accustomed to.

Leaving Benson to control his emotions, Tommy made coffee, placing a strong cup in front of the man. He needed it. "Do you know who the man is that your wife was involved with," asked Doyle?

Benson shook his head, replying, "I thought I did, but now I'm not so sure."

Scowling, Tommy asked, "What do you mean. Better still who do you mean?"

Benson hesitated, before voicing his superstitions as to who his late wife's lover had been. "Of course, he denies it," he moaned bitterly. "But I still think it's him."

"Are you sure," asked Tommy? Benson shook his head no.

"Okay leave it with me."

As Benson rose to leave, Tommy said, "One thing Mr. Benson. Why did you go for a ride in the gentleman's car the other day? What did you talk about?"

Benson turned, his face white with shock that Doyle knew about the meeting. He had vowed to remain silent on the subject.

"How, how, how do you know about that," he stammered in a whisper. "No one knows we met. I swore never to mention it. Oh dear, oh dear, what will happen now," and he collapsed into the chair he had just vacated.

Surprised by the man's reaction, and seeing his distress, Tommy quickly did his best to reassure him it was only by accident he had been spotted. However, Tommy was not satisfied, wanting to know more, so requested Benson take him into his confidence by telling all.

The man didn't know what to do. He wanted to trust Doyle but, him knowing all, could lead to worse things. 'What am I to do,' he thought. Staring for a moment he finally decided, confessing everything, which left Doyle in a quandary as to what to do next. Whatever he did he must not do it alone, He would need some good solid support to cover his back?

Eventually, Tommy said, "Do not worry about the matter, Mr. Benson. You have merely confirmed what I already knew. No one else will learn about anything that has passed your lips. Go home and say nothing to anyone. I will be in touch tomorrow."

Slightly appeased Benson left, clearly in a distressed state of mind. Once he had left Tommy rang the police precinct, asking his friend Mac to visit him at the earliest opportunity. After that, he sat back to plan a campaign of action.

Three hours later, Mac entered Doyle's office, an enquiring question on his face. Looking at his pal, he thought, 'Oh, oh. I know that look. He's up to something.'

"Okay, Tommy, what you got planned?"

Tommy looked at his friend, a hurt expression crossing his face, which only made Mac laugh. "Don't pretend to be offended, Tommy lad, I know you too well. So, what have you found out?"

Offering Mac a glass of whisky, Tommy began explaining.

Half an hour later Mac whistled, shaking his head in amazement, asking, "Are you sure about this?" Doyle nodded yes. "So, Tommy lad, what are we going to do about it?"

"It might be better you do nothing, Mac. You could lose your job if it fails," replied Tommy smiling.

Mac smiled back. Taking a swig from his glass, he laughed. "What the hell, Tommy, it has to come to an end someday. Any day will do. Besides, to be honest, I've had about as much as I can stand of Johnstone. One of these days I'm going to smack him." They both laughed out loud, knowing the feeling.

Having agreed on what to do, Doyle put together three envelopes, each containing a copy of the report and the photographs previously copied from the originals found in the drawer at the blonde woman's house. A few minutes later they left Doyle's office. They would meet again within the hour at their usual haunt - O'Malley's Bar. Both needed a good night before retiring as tomorrow was going to be a busy day.

* * * *

The next morning Doyle was up and out early. His first port of call was Benson's house where he advised the man to go straight to his attorney. He was to make any excuse he could but was to remain there until Doyle, or the police came for him.

Doyle's next visit was to the police precinct to talk to Johnstone. Despite not liking the man, he felt it only fair to forewarn him that all hell was about to break loose and that he was going to be involved.

Entering the squad room, he nodded at Mac. Everything was set up but, unfortunately, the Lieutenant was nowhere to be seen. Suddenly a phone rang; someone answered, saying, "Tommy, it's for you."

Doyle was not surprised; he had been expecting the call. Mac nodded too, being ready to listen into the conversation, as Doyle slowly placed the phone to his ear, "Doyle. Who is this?"

A smooth, quiet voice said, "Who this is, Mr. Doyle, is irrelevant. However, you will listen to me and take note. I have received an envelope with certain documents in it. What you expect to achieve I do not know, but if you do not provide me with all the copies you have, you will certainly regret it. Do I make myself clear?"

Doyle laughed, before answering. "And what makes you think the envelope was from me?"

The man sighed. "Oh, dear. I hope we aren't going to play games, Mr. Doyle. Listen carefully. You will do exactly as I say, or you will pay."

Doyle said nothing. Finally, the voice demanded, "Doyle, are you there, are you there."

"Yes, and your conversation has just been recorded by a very friendly police officer. A very good, honest, and truthful police officer, so I would be very careful what you say to me. Anyway, I have nothing more to say to you as I no longer have the copies. Would you like to know where they are?" responded Doyle.

"You lie," snarled the voice. "Where are they? What have you done with them?"

Doyle smiled, and as he went to put the phone down, he quietly said, "Why don't you turn the radio on. The news is going to be very interesting today."

* * * *

Two days later, Johnstone stormed into Doyle's office without knocking.

"Doyle," he yelled. "You bastard. How did you know who had done the murder; I demand to know."

Doyle looked up, deciding how to respond, before saying, "Ah… Lieutenant Johnstone. No sorry, I should have said… Officer Johnstone, shouldn't I." He paused, before finishing with, "Officer Johnstone… go to hell. I have nothing to say to you."

Johnstone looked at Doyle, hatred showing on every aspect of his face. He was just about to say something rather unkind when he was interrupted by the entrance of one Captain O'Riley who, in his strong Irish brogue, shouted, "Johnstone; get the hell out of here. You should be out on patrol, not minding other people's business."

The shock of the Captain's voice caused Johnstone to shut his mouth, and after casting an evil look at Tommy, he turned, quickly left the office, mumbling under his breath about getting even.

"Now, now, Tommy my boy, you will rile the man, won't you?" said the Captain. laughing out loud.

Tommy stared at O'Riley, a hurt look on his face. "Not at all, Captain; mind you he deserved it this time. And to what do I owe the pleasure of a visit from yourself?"

Just then Mac walked into the room, greeting his friend with a nod of his head, causing Tommy to say, "Ah, I see you've come mob-handed, Captain."

Laughing, O'Riley sat in a chair and pointing at Tommy, asked, "What I want to know, is how you found out who murdered Mrs. Benson?"

"Oh! Is that all? Well, it was good old-fashioned footwork... and a spot of Irish luck," he replied.

"Well, whatever," said O'Riley. "Tell me all?"

And Tommy explained why he couldn't believe the husband had killed his wife, especially as he could provide the perfect alibi. The fact Benson hadn't known he was following him had more or less convinced Tommy he was innocent, especially when he refused to name Gloria to the police. Finding the photographs, and the report had also helped him conclude that Mr. Benson was totally innocent in the matter.

What they did prove, however, was that Mrs. Benson was having an affair and that she had become a liability. Her lover was married, old school, old money, and was about to stand for congress. Although a philanderer for many years, something the man's wife chose to overlook, his affair with Mrs. Benson had become quite serious. Mrs. Benson had wanted to be his next wife.

What she didn't know, was that the money belonged to the current wife and that her husband would never, ever divorce her. They had been married too many years. He knew which side his bread was buttered, so to speak. The last thing he needed was a mistress with a big mouth.

At their last meeting, Mrs. Benson had tried pressuring the man, telling him she would tell his wife, and anyone else who would listen, about their relationship. He knew he could not let her do that so, he had arranged for her to meet with an accident. The young blonde Gloria was in his pay. She had deliberately set about enticing Mr. Benson into an affair, so as to get him out of the house, thus casting doubt upon his character; and setting him up for a fall.

Captain O' Riley sat listening, before asking, "And how did you get hold of the photographs and report?"

Casting a quick glance at Mac, Tommy thought, before responding, "I would prefer not to tell you that, Captain. I wouldn't want to incriminate myself, now would I?"

O'Riley laughed, nodding his head in agreement. "And now, Tommy my boy, would you be considering returning to the force. After all, you'd be working with Mac here!"

Doyle smiled, looked at Mac, and then the Captain, before replying, "Afraid not, Captain. Even though he's been demoted, I still couldn't work with Johnstone. I wouldn't be able to trust him ever again. But thanks for asking me."

The Captain stood up and holding out his hand he shook Tommy's hand firmly. Then saying goodbye, he left the room. Mac, saying nothing, saluted his friend, and turning, he followed.

"By the way, Mac, congratulations on the promotion," said Tommy.

Mac stopped - looking back he smiled, saying, "No; thank you, Tommy. I couldn't have done it without you. Meet you at O'Malley's later to celebrate."

"Sure, Mac, sure. Drinks are on you," and Tommy laughed warmly.

After Mac and the Captain had left, Tommy gathered his copies of the reports, photographs, etc relating to the Benson case and placing them in a file he wrote case closed across the top. Placing the file in the cabinet he decided to take a shower and get changed before going to meet up with Mac.

Later, as he strolled down the street he smiled to himself. He was still chuckling to himself at the sight of Johnstone being given a hauling over the coals. Life was good as a PI. Yes, life was good!

LONG LIVE THE DON!

The sirens passing the brownstone slowly dragged Doyle from a deep, dreamless sleep. Opening his eyes, he glanced at the clock; it said twelve twenty. He'd been in bed about eight hours, having only got in at four am.

'God,' he thought, 'I'm getting too old for these late nights. It's time I retired… again!'

Climbing out of bed he ambled across to the bathroom. As he washed his hands and face, he looked at his reflection in the mirror. He was getting old. Certainly too old to be doing the graveyard shift too often. Back in the bedroom he quickly changed, threw the covers over the bed, and left the room.

Having made a fresh pot of coffee, he lifted a clean mug off the drainer and poured himself a good helping of the hot murky brew; the smell assailed his nostrils with pleasure.

Leaving his apartment, he went downstairs to the office. It might be Sunday, the day of rest, but not for him; there was still work to be done, like making sure his paperwork was up-to-date. Sunday was the day he usually caught up with anything he had Missed during the week; a habit he had learnt whilst working as a cop.

Entering the office Doyle checked the answering machine; it was empty.

The sirens had long since disappeared, so the street was quiet and peaceful once more. Sitting at his desk, he picked up his pen and began making notes in one of the files. He had spent the last four days, no nights, following a wayward husband who was having a liaison with a local chorus girl. The wife had got to know about the affair but needed evidence in order to file for divorce. Doyle hated these types of jobs but hadn't had the heart to say no to the lady.

Anyway, the surveillance was over with now. He had the photographs which he would deliver, with his report, to the wife in the morning. Once the write-up was complete and the details handed over to the client the job would be finished.

'Thank God,' thought Doyle as he shut the file. 'Time for lunch.'

Leaving the office, he made his way downstairs. Stepping outside he felt the light warmth of the sun trying to shine through the clouds, on his back. There was a slight breeze but it was still warm enough to go without an overcoat. Strolling down the street Doyle whistled to himself. Ten minutes later he entered O'Malley's Bar and Diner, his favourite place to eat.

The bar was a small, family-run business, owned by Pat O'Malley and his wife Molly. They were Irish through and through. Pat ran the bar, whilst Molly worked in the kitchen. She was renowned for cooking a mean Irish-Stew and Dumplings - which just happened to be Doyle's favourite meal.

Stepping inside, he noted the place was busy; full of local families having their lunch.

"Hello there, Tommy. And how are you this fine day?" asked a deep Irish brogue.

Looking over to the bar, Tommy smiled, "I'm well, Pat. Can you squeeze me in for lunch please?"

"Now, when can we ever not find room for you, Tommy my boy," responded Pat. "Although, today you'll have to sit at the end of the bar if that's okay?"

"No problem, Pat," said Doyle, making his way to the other end of the bar to sit on a tall bar stool. "I'll have a long, cool one when you're ready, Pat, please?"

Pat poured a pint of the local brew, placing it on the bar in front of Doyle. As Tommy picked the glass up to take a drink, a soft Irish voice announced, "Now then, if it isn't my favourite PI, Mr. Tommy

Doyle. And were you not going to come and say hello to me then?"

Putting the glass back down, Tommy smiled, turning he discovered Molly O'Malley standing behind him, a big grin spread across her face.

"Well, hello there, and how is my favourite Irish girl?" he asked.

Molly giggled girlishly. "Oh, get away with you, Tommy Doyle. You're a fast talker, aren't you? Me a girl, I sometimes wish," and she winked at him.

Doyle took her in his arms, kissing her cheek, whispering, "You'll always be a girl to me, Molly O'Malley. So, what's on the menu today?"

Pulling away from him she pretended to frown, as if cross with him, but found herself unable to keep up the pretence, laughingly saying, "That's what you really like about me, Tommy Doyle; my Irish-Stew and Dumplings."

Doyle laughed in agreement. "But of course. You know the way to a man's heart is through his stomach. I'll have a double helping, Molly me darling. I'm hungry."

Molly laughed, and turning away, she returned to the kitchen, calling out, "One double helping of Stew and Dumplings, Tommy, just for you," and she disappeared through the kitchen door.

Doyle returned to his seat and picking up the glass, took a long swig of the cool ale. It was refreshing; he had needed that.

"Enjoying your Sunday off then, Tommy," questioned a voice.

Looking up, Doyle discovered his friend and ex-partner, Pete (Mac) Mackintosh, leaning on the bar next to him. "Hi Mac, what you doing here," asked Doyle.

"Called at your place, and as you weren't in, thought I would check here. Have you eaten yet," said Mac?

"Not yet. Do you want some?" asked Doyle. Mac nodded his agreement so Doyle popped to the kitchen door to order a second portion of Molly's cooking.

An hour later the place had quietened down. As Molly had finished cooking, she came into the bar, joining Doyle and Mac for a Drink and a chat. She was a cheery soul, who put up with a great deal from her husband Pat and her three sons; all strapping lads.

There had been some trouble in the bar when the O'Malley's had first taken it over. This was how Mac and Doyle had met the couple; responding to a call to the precinct. The perpetrators had come off the worse, having come up against the O'Malley clan in their full glory. They had taken no prisoners, and the three bruisers who had tried to twist Pat's arm for protection money had quickly learnt it would better to go away.

Doyle and Mac had smiled upon discovering what had happened, believing that perhaps in this instance, justice had been served, and choosing to take no further action. After that, the word went out that the O'Malley Bar and Diner was off-limits.

Peace had reigned ever since. Although occasionally, a new criminal would try to move into the district, he was soon put straight as to where not to go, or whose toes not to tread on.

Doyle's presence in the district over the last three years had also proven to be beneficial. The bad guys soon learnt they would not get away with anything as Doyle and Mac worked closely together, managing to keep the district as clean as possible. It had had a good effect overall, with new families moving into the area, making it a better place to live, and resulting in the bad guys quickly moving out. Businesses had prospered, people felt safe with a new community being born.

Later, after lunch, Mac and Doyle returned to the Brownstone. Sunday night was the 'guy's night,' when a few of the officers from the precinct gathered together to play cards. The stakes were low but it helped them unwind from what was a stressful job. This week, as it was being held at Doyle's place, Mac decided there was no point in going home, only to return a couple of hours later.

As dusk fell five other guys, besides Mac and Doyle were sat at Doyle's dining table, munching crisps and popcorn, drinking beer, and playing stud poker. The bets were a few dollars, but even so, Mac was on a winning streak.

"So, Tommy, what you been up to recently then," asked Bonzo, aka Karl Bonasozsky, Detective.

Tommy played his hand before responding. "Not much; a bit of divorce work."

"Geeze Doyle, that sucks, you should come back to the job," announced Curly, aka Charles Denver, Desk Sergeant.

Doyle laughed. "What and work with you lot of reprobates again. I think not."

The air was suddenly filled with pieces of popcorn, being thrown by the others, causing Tommy to laughingly yell out, "Hey, you guys cut it out; the cleaner doesn't come until Wednesday." They all laughed in response, throwing more popcorn at him.

The evening drew to a close about midnight, mainly due to most of the guys having to be up and at work by eight the following morning. Once they had gone Doyle tidied up, made himself a mug of coffee, and went off to bed, where he slept soundly regardless of his late-night drink.

* * * *

Early the following morning Doyle was up and had been working in his office an hour before his first client arrived. It was the wife of the man he had been following. She had come to retrieve the evidence of her husband's infidelity. Satisfied with Doyle's work she paid the bill and left, en-route to her lawyer's office.

'Another satisfied customer," thought Doyle as he filed the paperwork and locked the cash in the safe.

Suddenly the ringing phone blasted through the silent air. Picking up the receiver, Tommy announced, "Doyle PI Agency."

"Hi, Tommy." It was Mac. "You heard the news yet?"

Doyle surprised, asked, "And what news is that, Mac?"

Mac took a breath, before replying. "Don Grimondi is dead. Apparently, he died in his sleep last night."

"What," announced a shocked Doyle. "You kidding me, Mac? Hell, that's 'gonna put the cat amongst the pigeons. When's the funeral?"

"Not sure, Tommy. Will let you know. You going?" asked Mac.

"Might do; could prove to be interesting. What about you?" said Tommy.

"I'm with you on that one! Talk soon, bye," and Mac hung up, leaving Tommy to mull over the news he had just received.

* * * *

Four days later found Tommy leaning against a wall close to the bottom of the steps of the large Catholic Church. He was watching people slowly mount the steps. It was turning out to be the 'who's who' of the underworld; all were coming to say goodbye to one of the last old-style Mafia bosses; Don Giovanni Grimondi.

"Seen anyone of interest yet, Tommy?" Mac caused Tommy to jump at the unexpectedness of his question.

"Hell, Mac, you made me jump. And in answer to your question, I've seen everybody who is anybody."

Just at that moment, the funeral cortege pulled up at the kerbside. There were seven vehicles in total. The hearse was laden with flowers. As the funeral director opened the rear door six men stepped forward, ready to lift the coffin and carry it into the church. They were all known members of the Grimondi 'family,' one of them being the Don's only son, Jo-Jo.

The widow was helped from the second car. She was the deceased's second wife; Violet was her name. Aged only thirty-six, she looked like a model. Standing beside her were the Don's daughters, Maria and Carla; both older than the wife.

Doyle and Mac quickly sneaked into the church, taking seats in a rear pew where they could watch the cortege enter. The service was a long, drawn-out affair, and as it came to an end the pair quietly left, returning to where they had been standing earlier; ready to watch the scene unfold before them.

The coffin was carried out of the church and replaced in the hearse. There was to be a private service at the cemetery; the Don being interred in the family vault. Everyone else would travel to the Don's estate home. Doyle was going to follow them, whilst Mac returned to the precinct to check the video film from the blacked-out police van filming the proceedings. Mac wanted to see who was in town for the event.

An hour later, Tommy pulled his car into a parking space outside the Grimondi House. It was a grand building, screaming of big money; probably mostly illegal wealth. Mounting the steps, he entered the house but was stopped at the door by a big bruiser of a guy who snarled at him, "What you doing here, Doyle? This is a private event."

Tommy looked at the guy. He'd met many like him in his time; big guys who thought they were tough, yet underneath their rough exteriors they were soft pussycats. Hit them in the right spot and they would go down easily.

"I've come to pay my respects to the family," growled Tommy.

The guy took a step forward, saying, "Well, you've given 'em, so clear off."

Tommy waited, undecided whether to smack the guy or not when a voice interrupted them. "Hello, Mr. Doyle. Come to pay your respects?"

The two men turned to see who had spoken. It was Jo-Jo Grimondi, the deceased's son.

Tommy nodded his head. "I did Jo-Jo. I wanted to see your sisters. Tell them it was a very nice service, but this lug-head here seems to think it's not appropriate."

Jo-Jo laughed out loud. "Ignore him, Mr. Doyle. Come along, I'll take you to my stepmother and sisters," and with that, he turned away.

Looking at the bruiser on the door, Tommy grinned, then followed Jo-Jo into the room towards the settees where the main family was sat holding court. He took the opportunity to look around noting how many members of the different underworld families were in attendance.

Standing in front of the widow he shook her hand, making the usual platitudes of sympathy, before moving on to the daughters. He had known Maria and Carla since they were young girls. Both greeted him with warm smiles.

Standing up, Maria took his arm. "Mr. Doyle, come along with me and I'll get you a drink and something to eat." The pressure of her hand on his arm gave him no chance to refuse.

As they approached the table, where the buffet was laid out, she whispered, "Are you still doing PI work, Mr. Doyle?" Tommy nodded yes, as she continued, "If I came to see you could you do some work for me?"

He looked at her surprised, before answering, "What would you like me to do, Maria?"

She looked around, to see if anyone was listening, before whispering, "Shush, not here. Are you still in the same place?" He nodded again. "Then I'll see you in a couple of days," and upon that note, she changed the subject by asking how Mac was doing.

Getting the message, Tommy followed her lead, allowing the conversation to wander to his friend, before commenting on how well attended the funeral had been.

Half an hour later, feeling he had stayed long enough, he left the house with a final goodbye wave to Jo-Jo. A new Don was now on the throne. A new era in the Grimondi family was underway. Things might prove to be very interesting in the very near future.

Later that afternoon, Tommy met Mac at their usual haunt, O'Malley's Bar & Diner, where he told Mac about Maria's request for a meeting. Surprised by this, both wondered what it was all about, but until she actually told Tommy, they would have to wait to find out.

* * * *

Three days later the opportunity unexpectedly arose when Tommy, working in his office, heard the intercom buzzer sound. Checking the video screen, he saw the back of a well-dressed woman standing by the door. Pressing the button on the intercom unit he enquired, "Hello. Can I help you?"

Turning, the lady leant towards the intercom speaker. "It's me, Mr. Doyle; Maria Rizzo."

Quickly he pressed the button again, and with a loud buzzing noise, the outer door unlocked. Maria slipped in, closing the door behind her. As she did so, the inner door automatically opened allowing her to carry on through into the hallway.

"Come on up, Maria," Tommy called from the top of the stairs, "The office is on the first floor," and he watched as she mounted the stairs.

Leading the way into the office he offered her a seat. "Cup of coffee?"

Maria thanked him, accepting the drink and waiting until he had sat down before explaining her reason for wishing to see him. "The problem is, Mr. Doyle, I cannot get over the shock of my Father dying so suddenly. To be honest, I do believe he died before his time. In fact, both my sister and I think our step-mother may have had something to do with his death."

Tommy was surprised for this was the last thing he had expected to hear. The silence stretched out before he asked, "Are you sure, Maria? What makes you think so, and if she did, how do you think she did it?"

Taking a deep breath, Maria began explaining that her father had, within the last six months undergone a full medical examination. He had been told he was quite fit for a man of his age. But, over the few days prior to his death, he had suddenly been taken ill. The family doctor couldn't explain why, or what had caused this.

Her stepmother had insisted on the Don being kept at home. She had even brought in her own doctor; a young man called Matthew Jenson. Between them, they had managed to send the family doctor packing. Her step-mother had also persuaded her father to agree to his dismissal on the grounds that his doctor was past it, and out-of-date with modern treatments.

Tommy pondered all she told him, asking, "What does Jo-Jo say?"

Maria looked him in the eyes, shaking her head. "Nothing. He couldn't wait for our father to die. He's the head of the family now, the new Don." She paused, before practically crying, "Mr. Doyle, I'm sure my step-mother and this Doctor Jenson did something to my Father. I believe they know each other from some time ago but I don't know how to prove it. Can you help us please?"

Tommy looked at her. He knew there was no love lost between her and Jo-Jo, who was nearly ten years younger. Had women been able to inherit the position of Don, then Maria would certainly have been the head of the family by now. As it was, old Sicilian attitudes precluded her from having any involvement in the 'family' business.

She sat waiting expectantly for Doyle to respond.

Finally, he said, "Okay Maria. Leave it with me. I'll do some snooping around and see what I can come up with. What about an autopsy. Why wasn't one done?"

"She, my stepmother, vetoed it. She wanted to cremate my father's remains but Jo-Jo insisted he be buried in the family vault. She even argued with him over it but we all told her it was in Father's will; that he must be buried with my mother. Jo-Jo got cross about it so she dared not go against him. After all, he

64

controls everything now. I think she thought once my father passed that she would get her hands on his money, but that wasn't what he wanted."

Doyle nodded his head, before asking, "Just out of curiosity Maria, who does get the money?"

Maria looked across at Doyle, before responding.

"Well, apart from some minor gifts to others, Carla and I get a quarter each; my step-mother gets a settlement of three million dollars, and Jo-Jo gets the rest. We can all live in the house for as long as we want. Either way, it stays in the family, becoming Jo-Jo's home. I have been living back at the mansion since Freddie got killed, even though I still have the house we owned. Unfortunately, it has too many bad memories for me, so I have put it up for sale."

"Do you think your step-mother was expecting more than $3 million?" questioned Tommy.

"Oh, yes, Mr. Doyle, I am sure of it. You should have seen her face when the will was read. She practically went white with anger."

Tommy gave the matter more thought. "Okay, leave it with me, Maria, and I will see what I can find out. In the meantime, if I wanted to contact you how could I reach you?"

Maria took a card from her handbag, passing it across to him. "This is my mobile number. If I can't talk, I'll just say sorry, I'm not interested and I will ring you back later. I want to keep the matter quiet for the moment until you perhaps come up with something."

"Ok," he responded, and rising he showed Maria out of the building.

Returning to his office, Tommy mulled over the last hour and all that Maria had told him. It seemed very strange she would come to him and yet, in some way, not all that surprising as she had known him for many years. Eventually picking up the phone, he rang Mac, arranging to meet to discuss the matter of the old Don's death in more detail.

* * * *

"You don't think it's sour grapes, Tommy, do you?" asked Mac when they met later for a meal and a drink.

Tommy shook his head, replying, "I've known Maria since she was a kid. As she grew up, she realised what her old man was and tried to keep a distance between the family and herself; only spending time at the mansion because of her mother.

The fact she married Freddie Rizzo was down to her father. He wanted to cement the relationship between the two families. I'm sure she lost little sleep when he was shot. And I know she refused to marry anyone else, but I can't see her worrying about the loss of three million; she's a wealthy woman in her own right so doesn't need the money. No Mac, I think she genuinely believes her father was killed. The question is how to prove it."

Mac took a long drink from his glass, allowing himself time to ponder the question, before replying, "I suppose we could do an autopsy but would the wife or Jo-Jo agree to that."

Tommy shook his head no.

They were stumped as to what to do next. Finally, Tommy suggested, "Could you check this Doctor guy out, to see if there is anything in his past? I'll do some snooping as well, find out where he lives and works. Let's see if we can put something together that might help us prove one way, or the other, if what Maria suspects is true?"

Mac agreed to check the police files the following day, while Tommy would look at where the Doctor lived. Hopefully, between them, they could come up with something.

The rest of the evening the pair spent watching football on the TV back at Doyle's place.

* * * *

The following morning, Tommy spent his time researching Doctor Jenson. He appeared to be doing quite well for himself, as the apartment block he called home, was an expensive piece of real estate. According to the neighbours he had moved in only a short time ago, less than five months. They couldn't say what he did for a job, or where he worked, and they seemed genuinely surprised when Tommy suggested he might be a doctor.

Strangely, the more Tommy didn't learn about the young man, the more he wondered just who exactly he was. Finally, speaking to the landlord he found out something that went towards confirming what Maria suspected; that the widow and the Doc might somehow be in cahoots.

Returning to his office he rang Mac, letting him know what he had discovered. Mac arranged to call at Doyle's office on his way home, where they could go over what each had found out.

It was a few hours later that Tommy and Mac, sat in the brownstone office discussing all they had learnt about the young man so far.

"Well, a doctor he most definitely isn't," stated Mac. "I'm still waiting for a report from out of town, but in the meantime, here's his rap sheet," and he passed over a copy of the young man's criminal record.

"Five years for embezzlement," noted Tommy, looking at the record, "Do we know where?"

"Somewhere up state!" responded Mac. "It seems he tried to rip some old dear of her life savings to the tune of half a million dollars."

Tommy whistled. "Wow, that's not exactly peanuts, is it. No wonder he's gone for the widow. The Don must be worth millions."

"Yea, but if the widow only gets three million, and Jo-Jo gets the rest, apart from what the girls get, then we have to wonder if Jo-Jo is next in line for an accident?" questioned Mac.

Thinking about the situation, Tommy said, "Perhaps I should forewarn Maria about the guy."

"Might be an idea to get her to watch her back as well, but what about Jo-Jo?"

Doyle looked up. "They wouldn't be so stupid as to try to take him out, would they."

Mac shrugged his shoulders, raising his eyebrows in response, before continuing, "So what are we going to do then?"

Doyle sighed, while they weren't overly enamoured about Jo Jo Grimondi, they couldn't sit back and let Maria or Carla be murdered. What they needed was a post-mortem but how to get one done without raising suspicions. They were going to need some careful plans to sort this one out.

* * * *

Nothing happened for the next few days.

Tommy spoke to Maria, suggesting that she and Carla go away on a short break. When she asked him about Jo-Jo, he told her not to worry, he would keep an eye on him. But it would make his job easier if she and her sister were somewhere safe.

Reluctantly she agreed, saying they would return to Chicago to stay with their Aunt. It would be a good excuse, and not look too suspicious if they suddenly left. Within a couple of days, the pair had gone and Doyle breathed a sigh of relief.

By the time Mac had completed his investigations, he discovered that one Doctor Mark Jackson had trained in Canada, but having failed his finals, had never actually qualified. He hadn't, however, let that stop him. Crossing the border into America he had changed his name to Hanson, setting up as a medical practitioner, specialising in looking after elderly patients.

Over the following three years he had become beneficiary to some seventeen patient's estates.

Finally, the authorities had become suspicious after a local law enforcement officer began investigating the suddenness of the deaths in ten of the Doctor's patients. Doctor Hanson had quickly left town.

Moving further south, Hanson had changed his name back to Jackson, before setting up in practice once more; again, looking after elderly patients.

Following his previous practice, he had quickly ingratiated himself with his more vulnerable wealthy patients. This time, however, he had not been as fortunate, due to the unexpected return from abroad of relatives of an elderly lady he was trying to embezzle money from.

They had quickly cottoned on to what was happening to their Aunt, and before Jackson could react, they had involved the law. He had been arrested and jailed for four years. Being released early on good behaviour he had quickly disappeared again. By this time, the authorities further north, had begun to expand their investigations into all seventeen deaths where Jackson/Hanson had benefitted.

On the move, Jackson had changed his name yet again; this time to Matthew Jenson. Arriving in town less than five months ago he had managed to ingratiate himself into the old Don's household.

Where or when the connection with Violet, the Don's young widow had started, Mac wasn't sure. He was still awaiting further details, although he was positive there was a connection somewhere between the two.

"So, Mac," said Tommy, "what do we do now? It's obvious that he's practiced at helping his patients into the afterlife, the question is how to prove it."

Mac nodding his head, responded with, "The only way is to get an autopsy done. Whilst I would love to be able to convince the Chief it's necessary, we would still need a court order to do it and unfortunately, at the moment, I have no grounds for asking. Got any ideas, Tommy?"

Doyle shook his head as he too knew that a Judge wouldn't give an order without good evidence. They were stumped. Doyle felt disappointed that he wouldn't be able to give Maria any better news when he spoke to her at the end of the week.

As it happened, two days later, Mac got the ideal opportunity to press for a post mortem to be done on the old Don, when Jo-Jo suddenly became hospitalised with a mysterious illness. It appeared that one of his henchmen had come across Jo-Jo doubled-up in agony. They had rushed him into hospital where tests showed he had been poisoned.

Unfortunately, the doctors couldn't determine what the poison was as they were waiting the return of some results.

Maria had rung Doyle as soon as she heard about her brother. He had dropped whatever he was doing and had immediately gone to visit Jo-Jo. Mac, upon hearing the news from Doyle had joined him shortly afterward.

"So, what can you tell me, Jo-Jo? Do you know what could have caused the illness?" Mac asked.

Jo-Jo shrugged his shoulders, acting nonchalant, responding with, "No, Inspector I have no idea. Must have been something I ate."

"Something you ate, eh Jo-Jo! And who fed it to you, I wonder?" Tommy said laughingly.

Jo-Jo turned his head to look at Doyle questioningly, saying, "I don't know what you mean, Mr. Doyle. It was probably a scallop gone off."

Mac waited, then dropped a bombshell by saying, "And maybe you were eating with the wrong person, Jo-Jo."

"What do ya' mean?" snapped Jo-Jo sharply.

"Tell me who made dinner for you the evening you became ill?" asked Mac.

Jo-Jo thought before responding, "Not sure what you mean, Inspector.   Just what exactly are you trying to say. Do you think someone did this deliberately?"

Mac pondered, wondering how much to tell him. Finally, he said, "To be truthful, Jo-Jo we're concerned at the suddenness of your illness. Especially as it seems your Father was also taken ill quite suddenly just before he died."

Jo-Jo looked at Mac, surprise written across his face as it dawned on him that something wasn't quite right. He tentatively asked, "Are you suggesting my Father's death, wasn't natural."

"Not just suggesting. I'm telling you; I have a strong belief that he may have been poisoned."

"What," shouted Jo-Jo, aghast at the idea? He may have wanted to be Don but there was no way he would have had his Father killed just to achieve it. Now he was beginning to get worried, so he demanded that Mac find out who had done it.

An hour later, Doyle and Mac left the hospital. Before leaving, Mac had obtained a signature from Jo-Jo allowing an autopsy to be done on his late father. He also arranged for an officer to stand guard outside Jo-Jo's room, thus preventing anyone from entering without his express permission.

Within two hours, the guard had turned away both Doctor Jenson and the Don's widow; explaining that Jo-Jo was under police protection until further notice. The pair had put up quite an argument about the young man being Jo-Jo's doctor, but realising they could not gain entry to the room they had reluctantly left. Mac was notified immediately of their visit.

Four hours later, a Judge signed an order allowing the interred body of Don Grimondi to be removed from the family crypt and to be delivered to the county morgue.

Doctor Veronica Martin, ME, would perform an autopsy and all necessary tests to determine if foul play had been involved. Until the results were back, there was little else Mac, or Tommy could do.

* * * *

Two days later, the two men returned to the hospital. Jo-Jo Grimondi was about to be discharged. Mac wanted to know where he was going to stay for the next few days.

As it happened, he had decided to return to the family mansion. Mac wasn't sure that was a good idea, so Jo-Jo made a request.

"Mr. Doyle, my sister has great faith in you – and even though you are an ex-cop, I want to hire you?"

Tommy was surprised; taking a moment to ponder the request, before asking, "What about your own guys, Jo-Jo? You have plenty of muscle so why do you need me?"

Grinning, Jo-Jo responded with, "Yea well, they have the muscle but you have the brains. And with an ex-cop on the scene, well, no-one is going to mess with me, are they? So, what do you say, Mr. Doyle? Will you come and stay at the mansion for a few days; I'll pay you your usual rates?"

Tommy looked at Mac, wondering what would be best. Staying at the house meant he could keep an eye on Maria as she had returned home, as well on Jo-Jo. It would also give him chance to get to know the widow a bit better. Mac must have been on the same wavelength, as he nodded his head as if agreeing to the suggestion.

Turning back to Jo-Jo, Tommy agreed to the request, confirming he would nip back to his office, grab a few things, then join the family at the estate later. Jo-Jo smiled, pleased Doyle had agreed.

Four hours later, Doyle slowly pulled into the driveway of the Grimondi estate.

As he drew up outside the house, Maria came out to greet him. She was smiling warmly. "Welcome, Mr. Doyle. And thank you for coming. I feel much safer now you are here to protect us."

"No problem, Maria. When did you return?" replied Doyle.

Leading him into the house, she replied, "I came back earlier this morning. Carla decided to stay with our Aunt. They are going to Italy together at the end of the week. With Jo-Jo becoming ill, Carla said she didn't feel safe in the house. Anyway, Jo-Jo is in the study and is expecting you."

"What about your stepmother, and the young doctor," asked Tommy.

Maria looked around to see if anyone was listening, before replying, "The black widow is in the garden at the back of the house. We don't know where the Doctor is. He left three days ago and hasn't been back."

'Damn,' he thought. 'Perhaps the Doc's disappeared. Better ring Mac and let him know.'

Taking out his mobile he quickly dialled Mac's office number, telling him the situation. If the guy was in his apartment downtown then Mac might still have a chance to pick him up before he disappeared altogether.

Finishing his phone call, he turned back towards Maria, saying, "Okay, I'll talk to Jo-Jo first - then I want to look around the house. I also want to speak to whoever does the cooking."

Maria nodded her head before leading him through the hall and into the study where Jo-Jo Grimondi was waiting for him. Rising from the chair Jo-Jo stepped forward holding out his hand. "Welcome, Mr. Doyle, and thank you for agreeing to this. Is there anything you need?"

Shaking hands with the young man, Tommy sat in the chair and said, "Yea, Jo-Jo, I need to talk to the cook, and then get the layout of the house. I also need to know which room everyone sleeps in, and which of your guys I can rely on. I only want those who aren't averse to taking orders from me."

Jo-Jo smiled, replying, "Don't worry, Mr. Doyle. They'll all take orders from you, or they'll have me to answer to. Come on, I'll introduce you to them," and he left the room with Doyle following closely behind.

Down in the kitchen, Doyle had words with the cook, Mrs. Notaro. She was curious as to why Doyle needed to speak to her but relaxed, once she realised, he was not going to blame her for Mr. Grimondi's illness.

"Tell me," he asked her, "do you think you could remember what you cooked for Jo-Jo before he got ill? Also, I want you to think back to old Mr. Grimondi, and try to remember what you were cooking for him before he was taken ill?"

Looking at Jo-Jo, who nodded his head to indicate she answer truthfully, she took a deep breath, saying, "I didn't actually cook for Mr. Grimondi Senior on the day before he was taken ill; Mrs. Grimondi said she would see to it. As for Mr. Jo-Jo, I wasn't here the day he was taken ill. I had had a call from a relative to say my sister was sick. I arranged to go and visit her. Before I went, I made lasagne, Mr. Jo-Jo's favourite meal, and left it in the fridge for him."

Doyle's head shot up at this news. Just about to speak, the cook continued. "The thing is, that when I got to my sister's I found she was okay. It had all been a hoax."

"What," announced Jo-Jo, "why didn't you tell me this before now?"

The cook looked a little afraid but answered, "Because I didn't think it important. I just thought it was some kids messing about. Then you were taken into hospital so I completely forgot to mention it."

Tommy, wanting to defuse the situation, quickly interrupted. "Yes, well that's understandable, Jo-Jo. She was obviously worried about you."

The young man shrugged his shoulders, accepting what Doyle had said.

After explaining why he was in the house, Tommy turned his attention to the guys who worked for the young Don. There was some slight mumbling about having an ex-cop around, but a sharp look from their boss soon made them shut their mouths. They knew better than to disobey when Jo-Jo gave an order.

"Okay you guys," Tommy started, "I know you don't like me being here but I am, so for now you're stuck with me. My job is to keep Maria and Jo-Jo safe; just as much as it's yours. But we need a plan of action so this is what I want," and he began explaining what they would be doing. Once satisfied that they all understood the rules, Tommy and Jo-Jo returned to the lounge where Maria was waiting for him.

"Oh, there you are, Mr. Doyle. Is everything organised? Shall I show you to your room now?"

"Please, but first I want you to show me around the house."

A sudden knock at the door announced the arrival of a guy called Marco. As he entered, he asked, "Mr. Doyle, you wanted me to guard Jo-Jo?"

"Yes," said Tommy.

"Ah, come on, Doyle, I don't need a babysitter," laughed Jo-Jo.

"You will do as you are told," announced Maria. "I've already lost my Mother and Father. I do not want to lose my brother, so no arguing."

Jo-Jo grinned at Doyle, before responding, "Women! Aren't they bossy?"

Tommy laughed with him. "That's as may be Jo-Jo but she's right, and so you'll have Marco with you at all times; agreed?" Reluctantly the man nodded his head, allowing Marco to settle down in a chair near the door, while Doyle and Maria left to inspect the house.

An hour later, Tommy was settled in his room, and having looked around the house and grounds, in order to get his bearings, Tommy returned to the study to find Marco and Jo-Jo in the middle of a game of checkers.

As he entered the room, Grimondi, looked up. "Everything okay, Mr. Doyle?" Nodding yes, Tommy sat down to watch the two men playing.

The rest of the evening passed peacefully, without the widow joining them. She had disappeared to her room shortly after coming in from the garden.

Discovering Doyle in residence she was not impressed, and when she tried to object, Jo-Jo informed her Doyle was his guest. What she made of that was anybody's guess, although Tommy felt she was wary and uncomfortable with his presence. Of the young Doctor, there was no sign and the night passed without incident.

* * * *

Early the following morning, Tommy was up and about before anyone else had risen from their slumbers. Sitting at the breakfast bar in the kitchen drinking his morning coffee, he was surprised to discover the widow watching him from the doorway.

"You're an early riser, Mr. Doyle," she breathed in a soft, sultry voice. "Didn't you sleep well?"

Looking up, he studied her for a moment. Just as she was obviously beginning to feel uncomfortable under his scrutiny, he answered, "On the contrary, Mrs. Grimondi, I slept exceedingly well. Besides I always rise early; occupational hazard," and he returned to drinking his coffee.

Coming further into the room he noticed she was dressed in a slinky two-piece negligee in a delicate pink colour. 'So much for the grieving widow," he thought, carrying on drinking his coffee, and pretending not to have noticed her mode of dress.

"Why are you here, Mr. Doyle? What are you doing in my house?" demanded Violet Grimondi. Doyle didn't answer.

"It's not your house. And Mr. Doyle is here at my brother's invitation," announced Maria harshly from the doorway. "Good morning, Mr. Doyle, I trust you slept well?"

Violet looked at Maria. If looks could kill then the poor girl would have been laid out on the floor, stone-cold dead. Maria didn't move or say anything, she just stared back at Violet with a look of distaste on her face. The atmosphere was so thick you could have cut it with a knife. Tommy waited with bated breath to see what would happen next.

It was an anti-climax therefore when Jo-Jo suddenly appeared in the doorway announcing, "Well, I see you are up, Mr. Doyle. Have you had breakfast yet?"

Violet and Maria remained staring at each other in silent hatred, before finally moving away; both acting as if the venomous stares of moments ago had never happened.

"What do you want for breakfast, Jo-Jo... and you, Mr. Doyle?" asked Maria.

Jo-Jo was the first to respond. "Nothing, I'm going out for breakfast. Care to join me, Doyle?"

Tommy looked at Maria deciding it might be better to remain at the house, so smiling replied, "Thanks, but I'll give it a miss this morning if you don't mind?"

"No problem. I'll see you later," replied Grimondi, turning to leave the kitchen.

Violet quickly followed him, calling out, "Jo-Jo will you wait and give me a lift into town."

What he replied was not heard by those in the kitchen, but Tommy presumed it had been a negative response as Jo Jo left almost immediately. The widow departed some twenty minutes later in her car.

As he went towards the cooker, Tommy turned to Maria. "How about some breakfast Maria; bacon and eggs okay with you?"

Looking up in surprise, Maria smiled. "Sounds good to me. I'll make the toast and some fresh coffee." The next three-quarters of an hour were spent in silent companionship.

"There you are, Mrs. Rizzo. What would you like me to serve for dinner tonight?" asked the cook.

"Anything your heart desires, Mrs. Notaro. I am sure whatever you serve will be agreeable with everyone," replied Maria. Then turning towards Tommy, she said, "I'm going to get dressed, Mr. Doyle, and go into town. Would you care to join me?"

"Why not, I can call at the office whilst I'm waiting for you to finish your shopping."

And before rising to follow Maria from the kitchen he reminded Mrs. Notaro, "You won't forget to make sure you use new, fresh ingredients, and lock, whatever you cook, away until you're ready to serve it."

Mrs. Notaro had listened to Doyle the previous day when he had warned her to double-check everything in the kitchen stores as he didn't want a repeat of the illness Jo-Jo had suffered. She nodded her head in agreement, having taken his comments to heart after he had reassured her, she was not to blame for any of the bouts of illness.

The rest of the day Tommy spent in his office with Mac, waiting for Maria to collect him. He also learnt from Mac that young Doctor Jackson/Jenson had left his apartment three days ago, and had seemingly disappeared.

Unfortunately, no one knew where.

However, Tommy presumed the widow must know. He suggested that maybe Mac could arrange to have one of the undercover cops follow her, just in case she was in touch with the young man. Mac agreed, but in the meantime, he intended putting out an alert to other forces to be on the lookout for the Doctor.

* * * *

The next few days passed in relative peace.

Jo-Jo carried on as if nothing had happened. Maria spent her time between her own house and the Grimondi mansion. She also spent quite a bit of time with Doyle, telling him what she knew about her stepmother. As for the said widow, she kept a low profile; spending much of her time in her rooms, or out of the house visiting.

By the end of the week, Tommy was beginning to wonder if he had got it all wrong, and Jo-Jo's illness was just coincidental. He wasn't quite sure what to do next so was pleased when, later that morning, Mac arrived at the house.

"Good morning, Tommy. How are you liking living the easy life with the mob?" and he laughed.

"Very funny; but keep your voice down Mac, Jo-Jo is around somewhere," Tommy whispered.

Mac laughed. "Okay, keep your hat on. Is there somewhere we can go for a quiet chat?"

Nodding his head, Tommy indicated for Mac to follow him into the garden. Once outside he asked his friend, "So what have you found out?"

Waiting until they were a safe distance from the house, so as to ensure no one could overhear, Mac finally answered. "Yea. It seems that Maria's fears were not unfounded. The ME came back with the toxicology results. Whatever they used had almost disappeared from the Don's bloodstream, but it seems that interring the body in the family crypt meant it was cold enough to slow decomposition down. The drug hadn't completely disappeared. It was a fluke that Veronica found anything at all."

"Wow," exclaimed Tommy. "So, what's next?"

"Now," replied Mac, "that's where we have a problem. We can prove how he died but as yet we can't prove that Jenson, or the widow, was involved. That's why I'm here. I'm taking the widow down to the precinct for questioning but I need a favour from you."

Tommy stopped and looked at Mac. "Whatever you want, just tell me."

"Okay," Mac responded. "Here's what I want," and he went on to outline what he needed Doyle to do. Once satisfied that Tommy understood what was needed the pair returned to the house, following which Mac took the widow, under protest, downtown for questioning.

Once they had left, Doyle quickly carried out the small job Mac had asked of him. The results were a surprise. An hour later, arriving at the precinct he discovered the widow was ensconced in a room with her lawyer but would be questioned shortly.

"Any luck, Tommy?" Mac asked anxiously.

Grinning, Tommy replied, "Yea. I found this book. The relevant page is earmarked. I also found this," and he produced a small vial from his coat pocket.

"Mmm. What do you think was in it?" asked Mac.

"If the book is anything to go by something quite poisonous," replied Tommy as he turned to the marked page in the book.

Mac read the following:

Ricin from the castor oil plant Ricinus communis is a highly toxic, naturally occurring protein; a dose as small as a few grains of salt can kill an adult. The LD50 of Ricin is around 22 micrograms per kilogram (1.76 mg for an average adult, around 1/228 of a standard aspirin tablet/0.4 g gross) in humans if exposure is from injection or inhalation. Oral exposure to Ricin is far less toxic and a lethal dose can be up to 20–30 milligrams per kilogram.

"Geez Tommy, where the hell did you find this book?" questioned Mac

"In the widow's sitting room. It was hidden under the cushion of the window seat. The vial was at the back of a small drawer in her desk," he responded. "What do you want to do now?"

"Talk to the widow and find out what she knows about these. By the way, was anyone with you when you found them?" questioned Mac.

Tommy nodded. "Yes, Maria."

An hour later the two men were sat in Mac's office.

The widow had, of course, denied any knowledge of the book or the vial. Her lawyer was demanding she be allowed to go home but Mac was loath to let her go. The vial he sent for fingerprinting and the contents to be tested. If they matched the autopsy results then he would be able to hold her, possibly charging her with the death of the Don. The next forty-five minutes were long and stressful, but finally, the reports came through.

"It's positive," announced Mac. "The vial's contents match the poison used on the old Don and Jo-Jo. I've got a search warrant to check the whole house, but first I have to charge the widow. Let's see what she has to say, shall we," and he left the office, stopping in the doorway to ask Tommy if he wanted to join him. Doyle eagerly followed.

Despite the evidence, Violet hotly refuted all the charges; denying that she had killed the old Don, or tried to kill Jo-Jo Grimondi.

After another good hour of questioning, Mac called a woman police officer in who escorted Mrs. Grimondi to lock-up where she would be charged on one count of murder, and one of attempted murder.

By this time, a search warrant had been issued and Mac, Doyle, and a group of officers left the precinct with the intention of searching the Grimondi mansion and estate.

Arriving at the mansion, Jo-Jo was immediately on the defensive over Mac and the police entering the house. Once Mac thrust the search warrant in his face Jo-Jo had to back down and allow them to search the premises.

"Is this down to you, Doyle," snarled Jo-Jo at Tommy.

"No," Tommy snapped back. "But if it uncovers the poisoner, what are you worried about."

"Stop it, Jo-Jo. You know this has to be done. If Violet killed Father, then you should want to see her punished for it," shouted Maria. "We have to put up with the unpleasantness of having the police in the house. No insult to you, Mr. Doyle."

He smiled. "None taken, Maria. Mac will only look where it's necessary."

The room went quiet. Jo-Jo was fuming over the police being in the house. While Maria was concerned something untoward might be found, and Doyle was thinking about the young Doctor and where he might have gone.

A good hour later Mac entered the study to find the room in total silence. He waited a moment before speaking. "Okay Jo-Jo, that's it we're finished. If you want to see what we're taking away you'd better come through into the hall; you too Tommy?"

Doyle stood up, looked at Maria then followed Jo-Jo and Mac out into the hall. All the evidence they had collected was from Violet's rooms. It included a diary and a bundle of letters, which had been hidden behind some books on the shelves.

"What you going to do with that lot?" asked Jo-Jo with interest.

"If it's relevant we'll use it as evidence against Violet. Depends on what we find when we look deeper," responded Mac.

"You caught the doctor yet?" asked Jo-Jo enquiringly.

"Not yet, but it's only a matter of time. He may or may not be involved and until we talk to him, we won't know," explained Mac as he made for the door.

Tommy followed closely behind, picking his overnight bag up as he passed the hall table.

"Send me your bill, Doyle. I made a deal and I always stick to it," announced Jo-Jo as the two men left the mansion.

As they were about to climb into the car, Maria came running down the steps. "Mr. Doyle, thank you for your help. If Jo-Jo doesn't pay you, let me know and I will," and she smiled at him before standing on her tiptoes to lean forward and gently kiss him on his cheek. "Father always said you were a straight kind of guy; he was right. Goodbye," and she returned to the house as quickly as she had left it.

Climbing into the police car after Mac, Tommy settled in the seat. Mac looked at him, announcing, "I think the lady likes you, Tommy lad. Yea, I think she likes you a lot," and he laughed out loud.

"Drop dead," snarled Tommy, before cracking up himself with fits of laughter.

'Maybe Mac's right,' he thought. 'But the last thing I need is a relationship with a mob boss's sister."

* * * *

Despite the questioning and the pressure Mac tried to put on Violet Grimondi, she denied everything; saying the book was from the mansion library, and that she had never seen the vial in her life. The last bit she changed to, 'well, maybe she had seen it once and picked it up by mistake but that was all.'

When the fingerprint results came back, it proved she was a liar for not only were her fingerprints on the vial several times, so were the young Doctors.

Plus, the book had never been in the Grimondi library. Mac discovered that it was on loan from some place up country.

Finally, he had all the evidence he needed. Having her fetched to the interview room, Tommy watched, unseen, on the other side of the glass partition.

"Well, Violet, it seems that you have been telling me little porkers, haven't you," announced Mac.

"I don't know what you mean," responded Violet in that soft sultry sexy voice of hers.

"The results show, that not only are your fingerprints on this vial, but they are on it at least six times, which means you handled this little thing more than just once."

Mac stopped, allowing Violet the opportunity to absorb the information. "And another thing, you didn't realise that these days all library books are marked with an invisible stamp. Well, at least invisible until it's put under an ultra-violet lamp. Just like this one," and Mac produced a small lamp from a box by his feet.

"You see, Violet, when I shine the purple light on this page, just here, it shows where this library book comes from. And, as you can clearly see, it shows Taylors Falls. Now Violet, what do you think I discovered when I contacted the library there?" asked Mac.

Tommy had seen Violet's reaction at the mention of Taylors Falls. She had turned white and looked sick. 'Mac's hit a sore point,' he thought.

Mac waited for her to respond, but she didn't appear to know what to say.

94

"Now, how about you tell me where Matthew Jenson is. Come on Violet, it's not the first time he's killed, and unless we catch him, it won't be the last. And, if we don't get him, then you will take the fall for the whole sordid affair. So, what do you say? Help me, help yourself?"

Violet's lawyer was as shocked as she was at the turn of events. Leaning over he whispered something in her ear, before saying, "I think I need some time with my client, Inspector. Can we take a break while we discuss the situation?"

Mac stopped, wondering whether to continue with the interrogation or allow Violet time to gather her thoughts. He decided on the latter and rising from his chair, announced, "I'll leave you for a moment. Would either of you like a drink?"

Getting a positive response, he quickly left the room, organising one of the officers to get the pair something to drink, before going into the other room to talk to Doyle.

As Mac entered the room Tommy turned and said, "I don't know what you have on her but whatever it is, you certainly upset her."

"Wait and see, Tommy. I want to surprise you," Mac replied laughingly.

Half an hour later, Mac returned to the interrogation room, while Tommy observed the action from behind the two-way glass partition.

As Mac entered the room the lawyer spoke out, "My client wants a deal, Inspector."

"And why should I offer her one? What can she give me that I haven't already got?"

"I can give you… Jenson, Inspector," answered Violet in her silky voice.

Mac didn't immediately respond, but eventually asked, "And what makes you think that deserves a deal, Mrs. Grimondi?"

Violet looked at Mac and smiled before answering, "Because, I know where he's hiding out, and I can help you convict him."

"What sort of deal are you thinking of?" Mac asked the lawyer.

"Aiding and abetting whilst under duress. No jail time?" replied the lawyer.

"Forget it," Mac laughed. "There is no way she cannot do time for murder. The DA might reduce it to manslaughter, but I doubt it. Mind you, the DA would probably take into account if she were to help us catch Jenson, otherwise, I think it's first-degree murder regardless of whether we catch him, or not. That's the best I can do. Obviously, she knows where he is, and if by omission, she allows him to escape, then a charge of aiding and abetting the escape of a wanted murderer will also be taken into account and added to the charges. Think about it?" and standing Mac left the room.

Joining Tommy in the other room, Mac asked, "What do you think, Tommy? Will she tell us or not?"

"Probably; we need to know where he is, and quickly before he disappears completely," responded Doyle.

After another fifteen minutes, Mac returned to discover what Violet had decided to do. He was pleased to discover she was ready to co-operate.

Within the hour she had confessed to her part in the death of Don Grimondi, and the attempted poisoning of Jo-Jo. She also told Mac where to find Jenson. Having quickly despatched officers to arrest the man, they had returned some fifty minutes later with the Doctor in handcuffs.

"So, are you going to interview him, Mac?" enquired Tommy.

"Sure. Do you want to sit in?" Doyle nodded his head in agreement.

As the pair entered the interrogation room Jenson looked up, then away, as he spoke in a whisper to his lawyer.

"My client wishes to know the reason for his arrest?" asked the lawyer.

Mac looked at Tommy, indicating that he could take the lead, which he did. "Your client is under arrest for the murder of Don Grimondi, and the attempted murder of Jo-Jo Grimondi."

Jenson laughed out loud. "Murder, me, don't be so ridiculous. It was Mrs. Grimondi who murdered them not me."

"Do you know, that's exactly what she said about you?" replied Mac. "So, are you going to deny that you were ever involved then?"

"I do," replied Jenson cockily.

"Oh! Well, that's okay isn't it, Tommy?" smiled Mac.

Catching Mac's meaning, Tommy played along with what he was saying, waiting to see how the young man would react.

"In that case, my client can go then?" announced the lawyer rising from his chair.

Mac waited until Jenson had stood up before saying, "Well, actually, no he can't. You see we've sorted the Grimondi thing out but tell me one thing, what about the other deaths your client has committed?"

Jenson and his lawyer stopped in their tracks. Slowly the lawyer turned, saying, "What other deaths?"

"Oh," responded Mac. "You mean your client has failed to mention that his name isn't actually Jenson?"

The lawyer looked at the young man, a question on his face, before turning back to look at Mac.

"Yes, it appears that Mr. Jenson here, also known as Hanson, also known as Mark Jackson is wanted in three states, plus Canada, for a multitude of charges."

"Charges for what, Inspector?" asked the lawyer.

Tommy answered, "Not much. Just for causing the deaths of at least seventeen elderly people, and for benefitting from the proceeds of those deaths."

"Sit down, Mr. Jenson, you are going nowhere," finished Mac.

Two hours later the interview was over. Jenson had been taken down to the cells to wait to be charged.

Afterward, Tommy left the precinct, going to O'Malley's for a night cap, where Mac joined him.

Mac had remained behind to await further information from up north.

"So, what about Violet? She must have been involved in the murders?" asked Tommy.

"She was - more than we first realised. And by the way, her name isn't Violet it's Carrie-Ann Jackson," responded Mac.

"What," Tommy practically shouted. "Jackson, the same as the Doc's?"

"Yep. She's, his wife!"

"Well, I never," sighed Tommy in surprise. "Come on, tell all?"

And Mac went on to explain what he had learnt since Doyle had left the precinct.

"It seems that after Jackson's release from prison he had met Carrie-Ann, and they had set up house together, eventually marrying. Moving to LA, Carrie-Ann had been seen working in a bar by the old Don who had taken a fancy to her. She had played the old man well, believing that he loved her.

In order to be convincing, she had changed her name to Violet, going through with the marriage to him. Afterward, she and Jackson had devised the plan to poison the Don and take his money.

It was only after the will was read that she learnt she wouldn't get the money. Jackson had gone ballistic, shouting at her for not getting the old fool to change his will, and eventually convincing her to get rid of Jo-Jo.

At the last minute, she had had a change of heart, and instead of using all the liquid in the vial, she had only used part of it, which was why Jo-Jo had survived.

"Guilty conscience, do you think?" Tommy asked.

Mac shrugged his shoulders. "You could be right, Tommy. Anyway, Maria will be happy with the outcome, won't she?"

Doyle nodded. "True. That means being previously married Violet won't be getting the millions either. A job well done I think - cheers Mac," and he raised his glass in salute. Mac raising his glass in response.

* * * *

At the end of the week, come Sunday morning, Doyle took out the file marked Grimondi and began writing the final details of the case.

One day he would use the notes to write a book about his cases.

Finally, picking up the bill for his services to Jo-Jo, he studied it before tearing it into small pieces.

This was one time he could do without the money, and without any connection to the mob. Case closed for good, he hoped.

PERFECT IN EVERY WAY!

Doyle's week had been slow. He had completed his last case three days early and was beginning to feel bored. He hated having nothing to do, so was relieved when Mac (Inspector Pete Mackintosh) his long-time friend, arrived with a file for him to review.

Having poured them both a coffee, Tommy sat down, picking up the file Mac had placed on the desk. Opening it he quickly looked at the Inspector, asking, "So what's the problem, Mac. It's not often you bring a file for me to look at?"

Mac grinning, replied, "Wife is dead; she's old money. I'm not sure why, but I feel in my gut that the husband did it. Problem is, he has an alibi. Have a look at it, and then tell me what you think?"

"Okay," replied Tommy surprised that his friend was admitting to being flummoxed over a simple death. "Sum it up for me?"

Taking a deep swig of coffee, Mac began explaining the details of the case.

"Margaret Donnington was found floating in the river. Death by drowning, but the ME believes she was dead before she went in the water. Husband,

Martin Donnington, has an alibi; as do their two kids."

Pausing, Mac took another swig of coffee, continuing he said, "Wife left the house about eight pm, supposedly to meet a girlfriend. The neighbour witnessed her driving away. The husband was home but left about an hour later for his club where, he says, he stayed all night, only returning home about midnight. His wife still wasn't home by then, so he rang her mobile, got voice mail, and left a message for her to let him know if she was staying overnight at her friends. According to him, he then had a large whisky and fell asleep in front of the TV."

Mac waited for Tommy to assimilate the summary before carrying on. "The kids left about seven to go to a friend's party, staying all night. They left the party together, arriving home in the early hours to find the husband fast asleep. When he discovered the wife still wasn't home. Husband rang her mobile again and left another message."

"No reply?" Tommy asked.

"No," said Mac. "Regardless, they all went off to bed. At nine the next morning, having discovered she still hadn't arrived home, the husband rang the friend, who said she had not seen the wife last night, and then the local precinct. He got the usual spiel about needing twenty-four hours before reporting her Missing, etc."

"How did he react to that?" asked Tommy.

"How do you think? He went ballistic, ranting about his wife never going missing before; that her phone was off, and her not having arrived at her friends. Finally, the precinct had a local detective visit him to take particulars."

Doyle shuffled the papers, trying to find the detective's report, finally coming up with the page.

Mac continued. "About three days later, the wife's car turns up. It was spotted by a patrol car hidden in some bushes just off the road leading up to the viewpoint above the river. Now, here's where it gets a bit weird," and Mac leans forward to make the point. "The car was locked. Yet the keys were still in the ignition, and her purse was under the front seat! Other than that, nothing!"

"And nobody inside?" Tommy said, looking up.

Mac shook his head. "No. And no evidence to show misadventure, or anything else; although, a couple of the wife's hairs were found in the boot."

Doyle hummed to himself, before asking, "So, when did the body turn up?"

"About three days later. She was found floating in the river by a local fisherman. All the details, reports, and interviews are in the file. Have a read, Tommy, and tell me what you think?"

Sorting through the contents of the file, Tommy read the various reports and looked at the different photographs. Then he read the interviews with the neighbour, the husband, and the kids, as well as the wife's friend. There was also a couple of interviews from one or two other unrelated people who had known the victim.

Once Tommy had read the file through twice, he looked at Mac, whistled, before saying, "I see what you mean. The number one suspect should be the husband. Last to see her, other than the neighbour, but he appears to have a solid alibi."

The pair sat in silence, each lost in their own thoughts over the evidence, or lack of it, until finally, Mac said, "Maybe I'm getting old, Tommy and I'm looking for a bad guy where there isn't one? But, for some reason, my gut is still telling me to look at the husband. Or, maybe there was more to the wife than is obvious?"

After another ten minutes, Tommy finally stood up. "Come on, Mac it's nearly lunchtime. We both think better on a full stomach. Let's leave it for now and come back to it after we've eaten."

"Food, Tommy?" Mac laughingly responded. "Is that all you think about these days? "Okay let's go, but you're paying."

And grinning in response, Doyle locked the file away in his drawer before leading the way out of the office, and the building.

Walking at a steady pace the pair made their way to their favourite café, where they enjoyed a lunch of chilli. Throughout lunch they carried on an unrelated conversation, finally returning to Doyle's office an hour later. Grabbing a coffee each they sat down to try and resolve the case. Doyle re-read the contents of the file, this time including all the interviews.

According to the neighbour, the wife had driven out of her garage and down the street fast. He had waved; she had responded with a wave of her black-gloved hand. She had a mink coat draped around her shoulders and was wearing a large blue and white, veiled hat. Nothing unusual there, as far as he could see.

The neighbour had later seen the husband leave, about an hour after the wife. He had been returning home after walking his dog when he saw Mr. Donnington drive out of this driveway. The husband had waved to him, which had surprised him, as Donnington wasn't known for being so friendly.

Having read the interview, Tommy said, "According to the neighbour Donnington wasn't looked on as a very nice man; in fact, he appears to have been a bit of a show-off?"

Mac nodding his head, said, "True. It seems the neighbour was surprised that he had been acknowledged at all."

Tommy picked up the interview with the husband and began reading:

Mrs. Donnington had come home about five o'clock. She had been at a charity event during the afternoon. As she was going out, she had prepared a meal for the husband and the kids. The brother and sister had left for their friend's party at seven.

Mrs. Donnington had then gone upstairs for a shower, and to get ready for her evening out with a Mrs. Clarrie Burton-Smith, an old school friend. She left the house just before eight o'clock.

Mr. Donnington stated he remained in his home office doing emails, before getting himself ready to go out. He left the house about nine pm or just afterward and drove to his club. He stayed there until late, playing cards and chatting to friends.

Upon returning home, around midnight, he discovered his wife still wasn't home, so rang her mobile to find out when she would be back. Sometimes, she stayed out overnight, going back to sleep at her friend's house.

When asked if it was something she often did, he replied yes. But he was unsure how many times it had happened before, although he thought not many.

When the kids arrived home in the early hours, they had found their father fast asleep on the sofa. He was surprised to find his wife still not home, so had rung her mobile again. Getting the answering machine, he had left another message.

When asked if he was worried that she hadn't rung him, he responded that no, he was just annoyed with her for not letting him know where she was. The three of them went to bed believing she was at her friends.

It wasn't until nine the next morning when he was in his office that he rang Clarrie, the friend, only to be told Margaret had never arrived. That's when he got worried, ringing the local hospital in case there had been an accident.

With no record of her having had an accident, he decided to ring the precinct to report her missing. Unfortunately, getting the standard 'must wait

twenty-four hours before reporting her missing.'
Going to his office he had tried to ring her again but
received no response. He had then started pestering
the precinct until finally, they had sent an officer to
see him. He was sorry for ranting and raving at them
but he was very worried.

The officer had reported that whilst finding the
place in a bit of turmoil, there was nothing to
indicate foul play. The mess was partly due to Mr.
Donnington's secretary having gone away on holiday
at short notice. The other staff had not been pleased
about it.

Tommy looked up, asking, "Was the wife having an affair?"

"I don't think so. We haven't turned anything up to indicate that she was."

"What about the husband?" Tommy asked.

Mac thought for a moment. "No one has said so, but I got a feeling when I went to his office that there might have been some familiarity between him and the secretary." Mac paused, then went on.

"It appeared a couple of other staff members didn't like the idea of her going away like that. I got the impression that there is some favouritism where she's concerned."

"Does seem a bit peculiar, but you never know, could have been a family emergency!" responded Doyle.

Going back to reading the other interviews, Doyle picked up those of the son and daughter; they were quite similar. Neither had been able to cast much light on why their mother had disappeared. Their interviews merely confirmed the part about seeing their mother at home, them leaving for the party, the time they arrived home, and what happened afterward.

When asked if their mother might have been having an affair, the daughter had been particularly shocked, telling the officer that no way would her mother cheat on her father.

Turning to the interview with Mrs. Clarrie Burton-Smith, Tommy read that she had spent the afternoon with Margaret at a charity benefit, dropping her at the Donnington house about five. They had agreed to meet up later that evening at a restaurant in town.

Mrs. Donnington had later confirmed she would get there sometime between eight and eight-thirty pm. According to Clarrie, the wife had never shown. She had left several messages on Mrs. Donnington's mobile; presuming she was running late but she hadn't tried the house phone until around nine o'clock, getting no reply.

The next time she knew that anything was wrong, was when Martin rang her the following morning.

When asked if the wife might have been having an affair, Clarrie had reacted aghast at the very idea that such a thing would happen. Her friend, she had told the officer, loved her husband, regardless of his faults.

"So, according to the kids and the friend there was no affair," stated Tommy. "Where the hell does that leave us?"

Mac grimaced. "Up a creek without a paddle. The body was found about three days after the car."

Despite the facts, Tommy was beginning to think Mac was right in his assumptions about the husband. Unfortunately, with only gut feeling, there was no way they could prove it. The perfect couple, the perfect alibi and, it could well be, the perfect murder.

Reading the rest of the reports and interviews Doyle sat for some time thinking about the case, not sure how to proceed. He felt they were missing something but what?

Maybe Mac was right, they were both getting too old. The thought made him smile.

Suddenly Mac's mobile phone rang, answering it, he said, "Sorry Tommy, I got to go; needed down town. Keep the file, it's a copy so no-one will miss it. If you can think of anything I've missed let me know tomorrow. Right, I'm off. Bye," and he quickly left the office.

Doyle spent the next two hours reviewing, and re-reading, the file's contents until he had had enough. Locking the file away, he decided it was time for an evening in front of the TV watching football before retiring. Watching TV always helped him relax, besides giving his mind a rest from the confusion of a case.

* * * *

The following morning Doyle returned to his office, and having poured his third cup of coffee of the day, he took out the file, spreading the contents across his desk.

He spent the next three hours studying everything. By the time Mac arrived Tommy was ready to lay out the case before him.

Walking into the office, Mac asked, "Well Tommy, any luck. Have you come to any conclusions?"

Pouring a couple of mugs of coffee, then shaking his head, Tommy replied, "Not necessarily a solution; more like a number of unanswered questions. Let's start from scratch as if we were looking at this for the first time, and see if we can come up with the missing something I am sure is there. Okay?"

Mac sighed, disappointment showing on his face. "Okay, go ahead, give it to me," and he sat back, waiting.

Rising, Doyle took the photographs and pinned them on the wallboard he had installed for just such a use. As he did so, he explained, "Husband, kids, and wife's pictures, abandoned car, river scene, found body, etc. Okay?"

Mac nodded his head, saying nothing, letting Tommy continue. "Now, if we look at the husband; seems a normal type of guy. According to the file he owns and runs his own business, an advertising agency. It ticks over, but… he's not making a great living from it. As you said yesterday, the money belongs to the wife. She's old money; inherited it from her family. And, from what I can gather, she's kept a tight rein on it."

Doyle stopped speaking while he checked his notes. "According to the family lawyer, if they had divorced the husband would have got $2 million, kept his own business and all the debt that entails. But, he would have had to find somewhere else to live. She would have kept the rest, the house, and custody of the children while they are still underage.

The kids get a monthly allowance until they reach the age of twenty-one. They each have a substantial trust fund from their late Grandparents which matures then. And, they would have continued to live at the house for as long as they wanted to.

Although, I think she wanted them to stand on their own two feet. The lawyer told me she was very strict with the pair of them; making sure they understood the value of what they were to inherit. Both are planning on getting jobs after they leave education.

If the wife passed away the kids would get it all, and jointly own the house. The lawyer told me; Mrs. Donnington has tied the whole estate up very neatly; she was a very canny lady."

"OK," interrupted Mac. "So, let's just clarify the situation. What happens if she dies after getting a divorce?"

"Husband gets nothing, having already received the $2 million settlement," replied Doyle. "The kids get the same benefits whether Mom is divorced or not. However, with her dead, their father now takes control of the purse strings, meaning they don't get anything from the estate until their Father dies only their allowance.

The estate will come to them in the long run; or whatever is left of it, once the father has had his hands on it. He also gets control of their trust funds. The kids actually have more to lose by their Mother being dead. The question is; does that make a motive for murder? I doubt it. Besides, their alibi is solid. Fifteen plus witnesses verify the fact the pair did not leave the party until the early hours of the morning."

Mac thought about the summary while Doyle refilled their coffee mugs.

Tommy waited until he had sat back down before continuing. "According to the wife's friend, there was no lover. She was adamant that she would have known, and that her friend would have confided in her if there had been. We have to believe that what she says is true."

Doyle was silent, before continuing. "The wife was smart. Look at these photographs. Every event she attended shows her well-dressed. Her outfits were fully co-ordinated; speaks of class to me."

Interrupting, Mac asked, "Co-ordinated, Tommy? In what way?"

Laughing at him, Tommy shook his head, replying, "Matching, Mac. Wow, you don't know a lot about women do you; especially posh ones. The smart types want their outfits to look good, so everything has to be spot on. Whatever the outfit, the shoes, bag, gloves, scarf, and hat all have to match, or look right with the clothes she's wearing."

Looking back at the photo's he went on, "Even her jewellery seems to match what she's wearing. In all these photo's she wearing the same earrings; diamond studs with a small pearl droplet. And, in at least half of them, she's wearing a matching necklace. She's also got a diamond watch on, as well as her wedding and engagement rings."

Stopping speaking, he turned to look at Mac, asking, "Was she wearing any jewellery when she was found?"

Picking the file up Mac quickly read through the ME's report, answering, "No. There was no jewellery. No fur coat or hat either. Perhaps they were lost in the river?"

"Could have been I suppose," said Doyle.

"I suppose it could have been a robbery gone wrong! But what still confuses me, is why she was up at the viewpoint?" said Mac.

117

Doyle nodded his head in agreement, then taking a breath he started speaking again, "What concerns me, is what was so urgent that the husband needed to be in his office that morning? He doesn't mention anything important happening? So why not ring the friend from home? Also, why did the secretary go away so suddenly? It seems strange. When is she due back?"

Mac shrugged. "I'm not sure. Maybe we should go and check her out?"

"I agree," replied Tommy. "She might be able to throw some light on the matter."

An hour later, having called at Donnington's office, Mac and Doyle discovered the secretary was now back home, but apparently on extended leave until further notice. Mr. Donnington was not in the office that day, being away on business, so it was easy for Mac to obtain the secretary's name and address.

Pulling up in front of the small house where Sarah Compton lived, Tommy was impressed by the neatness of the place. Walking up the drive to the front door he noticed the garage doors were open, and parked inside was a smart convertible car. Nodding his head towards the garage, he said, "She must be well paid to afford a car like that, Mac. They aren't cheap."

Looking, Mac agreed with him, but at the moment that was irrelevant. Knocking they waited. When the door opened Mac, flashing his ID card, asked, "Are you, Sarah Compton?"

For a moment the woman hesitated, as if unsure how to respond, but finally replied, "Yes, I'm Sarah, can I help you?"

Mac quickly explained why they were there, and that they needed to ask her some questions. Reluctantly she allowed them inside; very reluctantly it seemed to Tommy.

Sitting on the couch, Mac began questioning her, "Can you tell us what you know about the death of your employer's wife, Mrs. Margaret Donnington."

Sarah responded that she didn't know anything, having only just heard about it since her return from holiday. She explained about her trip away and that currently, she was still on leave. As she talked Tommy watched her in silence, taking in details of her appearance. She was aged about twenty-five, blonde, slim-figured, and quite a good-looking woman. Clothes were smart, showing she dressed with care; another woman who liked to co-ordinate, even her jewellery.

Having completed his questioning, Mac stood up. As they went towards the open door to leave Doyle suddenly stopped, and turning towards Sarah, said, "That's a very lovely necklace and ear-ring set you're wearing, Miss. Compton. Most unusual. Have you had it a long time? I'd love to know where you got it from? I'm looking for something like that for my wife. What do you think Mac?"

Mac, surprised by Tommy's comment, turned to see Sarah automatically lift her hand and touch the necklace. Smiling, she responded nervously with, "Oh, these old things. I've had them for ages. They belonged to my Mother."

Mac looked a little more closely at the earrings. Suddenly it dawned on him where he had seen an identical set.

Shutting the door, he said, "I think, Miss Compton, you might like to rethink that last comment. Are you sure they belonged to your Mother? Can she verify that?"

Sarah, suddenly going very pale, became wary. Carefully thinking before answering, "I'm not sure what you mean."

Mac swallowing, told her, "Oh, I think you understand perfectly well. I'm going to have to take that necklace set for forensic testing. I believe they belonged to someone else. Mrs. Margaret Donnington! Under the circumstances, I am going to have to ask you to accompany me to the station, Miss Compton. Please get your coat."

Sarah, crying out with shock, ranted, "But, I've been away. I don't know what you mean. They were a gift."

Pulling something from his pocket, Mac held up his hand. "Miss Compton, I recommend you don't say anything else until we are at the station. In the meantime, please remove the earrings and the necklace and place them in this plastic bag."

Sarah was shaking. Feeling frightened, she slowly removed the items, placing them in the bag, then put her coat on. Before leaving the house, Mac read her the Miranda rights. Quickly they drove back to the precinct. Tommy, leaving Mac outside, returned to his office to study the file once more.

* * * *

The following morning, when Mac arrived at Doyle's office, he brought him up to speed about Miss Compton, and to give him a copy of her interview. She had been allowed to go home, once he had been satisfied that her alibi was genuine. Picking up the report, Doyle read that the night of Mrs.

Donnington's disappearance Sarah Compton had gone to the theatre with six friends. They had all willingly confirmed how she remained with them until midnight when she shared a taxi home with one of the girls who lived two doors away from her.

"So, what did she say about the holiday, Mac?" Tommy asked.

"According to her, she received a phone call from Mr. Donnington just before going out the previous evening. He told her he had won a holiday but couldn't take it at such short notice. Rather than lose the holiday he asked her if she would like to go in his place. She had only agreed to go after he had reassured her it was okay to take a friend with her, which she had. The following morning, they left early, boarding the ship at ten am. It sailed later that day.

With all the excitement and rush of things she hadn't seen the news, so didn't find out about Mrs. Donnington until after she returned," explained Mac.

"Well, well, well," responded Doyle. "Okay; but what about the jewellery?"

"Now that is interesting. It seems she and Donnington started having an affair about three or four months ago. He gave her the jewellery as a gift. The test results aren't back yet but I'll bet you money it will show they are the ones belonging to Margaret Donnington. They were made especially for her fiftieth birthday. I asked Sarah when had he given them to her?"

"And what did she say?" asked Doyle.

Mac replied, "She said she couldn't remember but she has had them for quite a few weeks."

"Hang on, Mac. Something doesn't make sense here," announced Doyle, and picking up the newspaper he had been reading that morning he opened it at the social pages. Then, rising from his desk he went over to the notice board where the photographs were still pinned up to compare the newspaper picture to them.

"Have you found something, Tommy," asked Mac.

"I think I have. Yea, I do believe I have; hang on a sec," and returning to the desk he looked through the file of papers.

Finally, he pulled out the forensics report on the car, and smiling, he looked at Mac, saying, "Eureka. He could only have given her the jewellery that night or the following morning. If her alibi is solid, and he didn't see her that night, then he took the jewellery to her the following morning. Now, if she's lied, and he gave her the jewellery the previous evening, then her alibi isn't as solid as we think it is."

Mac looked at Doyle, a puzzled expression on his face. "Okay, Tommy, you have the floor, explain," and he sat back to wait patiently whilst Tommy double-checked the details.

Once he was happy, Tommy began explaining. "Right, this is what I believe may have happened. The wife spends the day at the charity benefit. She arrives home, removes her outfit as she is going to cook. She will change later before going out to meet her friend. Now, these photographs tell us that she was a smart dresser; that everything she wore went well together. They also tell us that she had a particular favourite piece of jewellery; the diamond and pearl set, which it appears she wore all the time.

Having made the kids and her husband something to eat, Margaret goes to get showered and changed. However, she has plenty of time so decides to have a bath instead. Now, there is no way a woman like her would take a bath or a shower in her jewellery. So, she removes it, if she hasn't already done so earlier."

Tommy paused to think for a moment, before continuing.

"Throwing a spanner in the works, what I do wonder, is whether or not Mrs. Donnington knew at this point that her husband had started the affair. I can't rightly say. She may have done and not been bothered; after all, she held the purse strings so could easily keep him in line. Or, she might have had enough of his philandering. I am sure this isn't the first time he's strayed. Maybe finally, she puts her foot down, telling him she wants a divorce. This bit is all speculation, of course, unless the husband confirms it."

Doyle stopped speaking, watching Mac nodding his head in agreement, before going on. "Either way, let's say, for some reason the husband snaps and filled with rage he goes into the bathroom where he holds her head under the water. Drowning her in the bath."

"Hang on, Tommy. You forget the neighbour. He swears he saw her leave, and that she waved to him," announced Mac.

"True," Tommy agreed. "But I bet it wasn't Mrs. Donnington he saw in the car. What if it was Mr. Donnington."

"What," Mac almost shouted. "How the hell do you work that one out?"

Doyle held up his hand indicating Mac should calm down, saying, "Read what the neighbour said," and Doyle passed Mac the report.

"According to him, he saw a blue and white hat, a fur coat, and a black-gloved hand. And, she was driving fast. A lot faster than she normally did, which was why he noticed her," said Mac out loud.

"The thing is, that nowhere, does he actually say, he saw her face, or that she turned to look at him! So, let's presume it wasn't her, but Mr. Donnington. He drowns her in the bath, dries, and dresses her in the outfit she has already laid out ready for the evening. Once she is dressed, he takes her down to the garage and puts her in the boot of her car. He takes the blue and white hat and fur coat, but he can't wear her gloves. Why? Because his hands are too big, so he uses his own. He gets into the driving seat, draping the fur coat around his shoulders. From a distance, it looks like Mrs. Donnington is driving, especially if she's driving fast."

Tommy stops speaking, asking Mac, "Are you with me so far?"

Mac nods, saying nothing.

Pointing at the photographs, Tommy continues. "If you notice, whenever she wore the blue outfit, she always wore a blue and white hat, white shoes, and white gloves!" Doyle stops to allow this thought to sink into Mac's mind. As he watches his friend's face, he notices how the idea of how the murder was committed slowly begins to dawn on him. Then he continues, "As far as anyone is concerned the husband has an alibi, being at home after the wife left."

"No hang on Tommy. I think you are forgetting something," said Mac picking up the husband's interview report. "According to Donnington, he was on the internet sending emails to clients. The records show that these were sent at the time he says they were."

Doyle looks at Mac questioningly, before remarking, "And I thought I was the one who couldn't understand technology. For your information, you can write your emails days before you send them. Part of the programme allows you to set the send date on emails so they can go automatically at a later time or date. Let's say the husband wrote the emails earlier in the day but set them so they didn't actually go until say eight-thirty pm? How would you know? You wouldn't because there's no way to prove it."

"Wow," said Mac, "that's a new one on me. But wait a minute, surely the written email would show the time and date he wrote it, after all, emails are practically instant. You can't mess with that can you?"

Doyle smiles, "Well yes, you can. All you have to do is change the date and time on your computer."

A surprised look had appeared on Mac's face, so Tommy explains. "Right, let's say Donnington sits at his computer to write an email. The date on the email shows it having been written at that date and time. Okay?" Mac nods that he understands. "But what if he changes the date and time on the computer, before writing the email, to the day following. He puts the email in the outbox ready to send the following day at the same time. The recipient will find that the date and time shown, matches that of when it is received. All Donnington has to do then, is to change his computer back to the original date and time."

"Wow, Tommy, that's a good one. Carry on mate, you're doing quite well so far, but you still haven't shown me how he did it," and he smiled, to show there was no sarcasm intended.

Taking a deep breath, Tommy went on. "Okay. Donnington, now dressed as the wife, takes her car up to the viewpoint. All he has to do is throw her body over the parapet into the river below. Goodbye, Mrs. Donnington. Driving reasonably fast but within the speed limits so as not to draw attention to himself; it would take him about fifteen minutes to get to the point."

"So really, he would need an accomplice," interrupted Mac.

"Maybe," agreed Doyle.

"But what if he was alone," asked Mac.

"Well," answered Tommy, "let's say five minutes to dump the body and lock the car, meaning he would have about forty minutes to get back home, get ready, and leave just after nine. Mmm… He could make his way down the hill or get down to the river bank, then run along it until he was far enough away to pick up a cab. He gets it to drop him off not far from the house.

Maybe he sneaked in over the back-garden fence and in through the back door. He couldn't risk going in the front way. He then gets a quick shower and leaves just after nine o'clock for his club, missing the phone call from the wife's friend. Of course, this is all speculation, unless we can prove differently."

Suddenly Mac's mobile began ringing. Taking it from his jacket pocket he quickly answered the call. Once finished he turns to Doyle, saying, "That was forensics. The jewellery was Mrs. Donnington's; having her DNA all over it. I think it's time I had

129

another word with Miss Compton. Let's see if she will confirm when she actually did get the set. Sorry Tommy, carry on."

"Okay. Talking about the jewellery. The one thing the husband wouldn't want to do is get rid of it. After all, it must be worth quite a bit, and besides, he has a nice good-looking young woman to give it to."

Mac holds his hand up, asking, "True, but what about the coat? What happened to that?"

Doyle thought for a moment, before responding, "Mmm; he couldn't take it home with him. And having already dumped the body all he could do was leave it in the car. Unless of course, he had already locked the door with the keys inside! So, perhaps he threw the coat in the river, along with the hat and gloves. Did the guys trawl the river bank for any of those items?"

Picking up the report of the action taken on the day the body had been found, Mac said, "According to the report, no coat or hat; but an odd black glove was discovered. As it was a man's it was discounted as being evidence. Damn, her gloves!" yelled Mac. "What the hell happened to the gloves?" He returned to the forensics list to see if they had been found.

"Hell, they didn't find them. And, they didn't keep the man's glove either," he said.

"It could mean her gloves are still there? We need to get them to search again, and quick," announced Doyle.

Picking up his mobile, Mac rang the precinct, arranging for a couple of patrolmen to go along to the river bank to look for the white gloves and the odd black one. He told them he would join them shortly. "Okay, Tommy, finish it and then we'll get off."

Doyle paused before completing his explanation. "Having got back home, Donnington showered, got ready, and went to his club, making sure the neighbour saw him leave. He may have known what time the neighbour took his dog out so timed it just right; waving to make sure he was seen, thus giving him an alibi. That's it, Mac, what do you think?"

Standing up, Mac said, "Phew. I agree with all you've suggested. Let's get over to the river to see if we can find those gloves and the hat."

An hour later, Mac and Doyle sat waiting impatiently for the results of the search. So far there'd been no luck in finding the gloves, coat, or hat. They were beginning to despair when Doyle suddenly noticed an old woman tramp, watching them from a distance. He recognised who it was and going towards her, he said, "Hello Meg, how you doing?"

Old Meg looked warily at Doyle, her eyesight wasn't as good as it used to be, so it took her a moment or two to recognise him.

Once she had, she replied, "Hello, Mr. Doyle. What's happening here?" nodding her head towards the police officers searching the river bank.

"We're looking for some old clothes, Meg; a fur coat, blue and white hat, and some lady's white gloves and an odd man's black glove. You wouldn't happen to have seen anything like that would you?" asked Doyle wishfully; not holding out much hope.

Thinking for a moment, Old Meg finally asked, "Are they worth anything, Mr. Doyle?"

Mac, having heard the conversation, said, "Depends. They could be worth something if they're the right ones. Have you seen anything similar, or do you know where they might be?"

Old Meg cast a sly look towards the pram she pushed around in which she kept her belongings hidden.

Doyle catching the look, asked, "Meg, do you have them, or something like them in your cart?"

"I didn't steal them, Mr. Doyle. I found them, and if people throw things away that they don't want anymore, then it's not a crime if I rescue them, is it?" stated Meg, all the while shaking, thinking she had done something wrong.

"No, it isn't a crime," replied Mac. "And, you can't get into trouble."

"But, if you have something that could solve a murder, then you have to say so and show us what you have, don't you?" finished Tommy.

Old Meg looked at Doyle, then at Mac, and back at Doyle, before finally making up her mind. Lifting the newspapers from the cart she showed them a fur coat, blue and white hat, something that had once been a pair of lady's white gloves, and an odd gent's black glove neatly folded in the bottom of the pram.

Mac couldn't believe his eyes. Signalling one of the officers he had the items bagged and sent to forensics. Old Meg was not happy at losing her prized possessions but, she was honest and wouldn't lie. Especially not to Mr. Doyle. He had always treated her well and with some respect, regardless of her being a bag lady.

Mac asked her how she had come to rescue the clothes and she explained she had been scavenging one evening when they had fallen from the sky, so she had gathered them up. Then she had heard someone sliding down the hill so had quickly hidden behind some bushes. Neither Mac nor Doyle could believe their luck.

Tommy asked, "Did you see the man's face, Meg?"

Unfortunately, it had been too dark and she had not seen the man, much to Mac's disappointment. But, having the clothes was better than nothing. As they were about to leave, Tommy turning to Mac, asked, "How much money you got on you?"

Putting his hand in his pocket, Mac pulled out forty dollars. Doyle, checking his pockets came up with forty-five dollars. Keeping ten dollars each, they pooled the money, and going over to Meg, he pressed the money into Megs' hand, telling her, "Take this Meg, for the clothes. Go and stay at the hostel and get something to eat."

She looked at the money, and a smiling, toothless grin crossed her face. "Thank you, Mr. Doyle. You're a real gent, you are," and turning away she pushed her pram down the pathway and was soon lost from sight.

"Will she go?" asked Mac.

"Probably not, but she'll make good use of the money. Thanks, Mac," replied Tommy.

"No worries," and the two of them returned to Doyle's apartment for the evening.

* * * *

Two days later Doyle received a phone call. It was Mac asking him if he would like to listen in on the interview with Martin Donnington. "Yea, why not, should prove interesting. See you in an hour."

At the precinct, Doyle watched through the two-way mirror whilst Sarah Compton was interviewed. After some time, she finally confessed that Donnington had given her the jewellery on the evening before she left for the cruise. She had been out at the time he called but he had left a message telling her it was a special gift. She had, of course, been delighted. There would be no further action against her, although she was given a warning for not telling Mac about the jewellery at her previous interview. She admitted she had been frightened, thinking Martin had taken the jewellery without permission. She hadn't wanted to get him into trouble.

The interview with Donnington went on for a while. He continued denying the whole affair; even after Mac had told him about the discovery of the clothes. It seemed Donnington was going to try and brave it out. Much later, he would change his mind; once the DNA proved that the clothes belonged to his wife and the odd black glove to him.

The reason he had snapped had been much the way Tommy had predicted. The wife had finally had enough of his philandering; demanding a divorce. He hadn't wanted to give her one as he knew he would lose out financially. As it turned out he had now lost everything; business, money, and his children. They would never speak to him again or forgive him for murdering their mother.

Back in his office Doyle gathered up the papers and returned them to the file. He then placed it in the cabinet where he kept all his closed cases.

One day he was going to write about his life and these cases. 'They'll make a good story for the book,' he thought, and he closed the door of his office for the night.

Another case closed.

ONLY HUMAN

The phone was ringing in the office as Doyle let himself into the building. Climbing the stairs, he was tempted to ignore it, but the persistent way in which it rang, called out to him. 'Answer me now' it seemed to be saying.

Opening the office door, he crossed to the desk and picked the receiver up. "Doyle Investigations."

There was no reply, just silence.

About to replace the receiver, he stopped as a timid voice said, "Mr. Doyle. I need your help." It was an older man. At least he sounded older.

"And how can I help you, Mr. err?" Doyle asked.

There was hesitation, before the man said, "I'm being black mailed, and I don't know what to do. Can you help me?"

Doyle thought for a moment, before replying, "Can't you go to the police?

There was a short pause. "I cannot do that," the gentleman explained. "The matter is very delicate, and the outcome would hurt someone else. Do you think you could help me, please? I can pay you for your time."

Doyle sighed. "Can you come to my office in the morning? I'll need to meet you and get more information. Say about ten o'clock?"

There was silence as the man thought about it. Finally, he said, "Okay, I'll be there at ten. Thank you, Mr. Doyle," and the caller hung up, leaving Doyle listening to the dialling tone.

Putting the phone down Tommy left the office and went upstairs to his apartment. He wasn't sure what to make of the call. Mind you, it wasn't the first time he'd helped someone being blackmailed. To be honest this was one part of his business he disliked the most. Basically, because he hated with a passion, the perpetrators of such actions. There was little he could but leave it until tomorrow.

* * * *

The following morning, about ten o'clock, Doyle heard a gentle knock. Opening the office door, he found a slightly built man Dressed in a smart suit and overcoat, holding a hat in his hand. He stood silently waiting to enter. Doyle put his age at about sixty. He also seemed very nervous.

Moving to one side, Doyle said, "Come in. Take a seat. I'm Tommy Doyle. You rang me last night about blackmail, yes?"

138

Passing into the room, the man sat, finally managing to say, "Yes. I did, Mr. Doyle. Can you help me?" He appeared to be extremely nervous. Doyle realised he would have to tread carefully.

Offering the man some coffee, he refused.

Having poured a mug for himself Doyle sat down in his chair on the other side of the desk, then asked, "So, tell me, what do I call you?"

Swallowing hard, the gentleman looked around the office, then a quiet, timid voice said, "Merton. My name is Phillip Merton."

"Okay, Mr. Merton," replied Doyle. "Tell me, why are you being blackmailed, and by whom?"

It was obvious to Tommy that Mr. Merton didn't know where to start; probably due to him being embarrassed by whatever it was that had left him vulnerable to such an action.

Doyle gave him a moment or two to gather his thoughts, before saying, "Phillip, can I call you Phillip?" The man nodded in agreement. "I know you are probably feeling awkward about sharing with me your personal problems but, if I am to help you I will need you to be as honest and as truthful with me as you can. Whatever you say will not go beyond these four walls. Think of me like you would your doctor, or your lawyer. Full confidentiality. Just remember, you must tell me everything, okay?"

Looking across the desk, Merton must have seen the sincerity in Tommy's face and eyes so, taking a deep breath, he began explaining what had happened that had led to his current predicament.

Phillip explained how he had lived in town most of his life. Whilst still married, he and his wife had Drifted apart, which led to them having separate lives. Life had not been that good for him until about nine months ago when he had met a delightful young woman called Annabel.

"Oh! I know I was probably stupid, Mr. Doyle, after all, she is some fifteen years younger than me, but she is... was... a lovely girl," and he paused. "I am afraid I fell for her," and he smiled sheepishly at the confession.

Doyle smiled back, saying, "You are not the first gentleman to be taken in by a pretty face, and I am sure you won't be the last. Tell me, what went wrong?"

"That obvious," replied Mr. Merton. Doyle nodded, waiting for him to continue.

"I thoroughly enjoyed the experience. Annabel made me laugh and feel good about myself. In fact, I was ready to leave my wife for good; ask her for a divorce. Everything was going fine, until recently. One day my wife announced that she had terminal cancer. What was I to do? I was confused. I just felt unable to leave her at this time. So, I told Annabel I had to break our relationship off."

"And how did the young lady take the news?" asked Doyle.

"She was not pleased. In fact, she was quite distressed, but then, after reassessing the situation she appeared to understand my reasons and accept my decision. I thought everything was okay. That was until about a month ago when I got some rather compromising photographs through the post," and he blushed profusely if that is at all possible for a ruddy-faced man to do?

"I don't know how or when they were taken. I thought Annabel loved me, daft as it sounds. That she really cared for me, and that eventually, we would be together. Now... I feel so foolish." His voice trailed off as once more he was filled with embarrassment, and there were tears in his eyes as the feelings of betrayal hit him once more.

"Right, Phillip... Mr. Merton," said Doyle. "Firstly, I need you to tell me is it Annabel who is blackmailing you?"

Looking up in surprise, Merton replied, "Oh no, it's not Annabel. At least, I don't think it is. To be honest I cannot tell. All I know is that I have been asked for twenty thousand dollars. But I haven't got that sort of money to spare, especially with my wife needing treatment. What am I to do? Do you think you can assist me, Mr. Doyle?"

Doyle sighed. He saw no reason why not. "I'm sure I can. Err, not wanting to embarrass you I am a fraud I do need to know if you have brought the photographs with you? And was there a note included?"

"Yes," responded Mr. Merton, "there is one inside," and, with some slight reluctance, he passed over a large manila envelope.

Sliding the photographs from the envelope, Tommy put the note to one side and studied the images. Having looked at them he picked up the note by the corner and read the contents. It was an A4-size piece of paper. The message had been made up from letters cut from old newspapers and magazines.

It read: These are copies. We want 20 thousand dollars. Will contact you with the details. Pay up or the wife gets the pics.

Doyle was annoyed by the note. He didn't like blackmailers.

Carefully he placed the note inside a plastic folder. He would ask Mac to check for fingerprints. Criminals didn't realise, that these days, it was often quite easy to get fingerprints from paper. Having placed it in the plastic folder he took it to the photocopier, copying the sheet for his files.

Returning to his desk, Doyle asked, "Phillip, when do they want you to hand the money over?"

Looking at him, Mr. Merton said, "I don't know. I haven't heard anything more since. What shall I do Mr. Doyle?"

Thinking about it for a moment, Tommy told him, "Okay, the first thing we do is get as much detail down as possible. I will need Annabel's full name, address, and where you met her. We also need to get you finger printed."

"What for?" asked Merton, shocked by the suggestion.

"To eliminate your prints from any we find on the paper. If we can find out who has been doing this, we will need the evidence to prosecute them," responded Doyle.

"What. I don't want to prosecute Annabel. She can't be involved in this. Besides, I err, I don't know her full name and address. I never thought to ask her," he responded, aghast at the very idea of her being involved. And yet, suddenly, he began to realise it might just be possible. After all, he didn't know very much about her. What an old fool he had been.

It suddenly dawned on Doyle, that he might have problems with the man unless he could make him understand exactly what he had got himself involved in. Taking a deep breath, he decided to speak firmly. "Now look here, Mr. Merton, I don't think you fully understand what a mess you are in. Whether you want to admit it or not, this Annabel is certainly involved in the affair, somehow."

He paused before going on, "How do you think they got these photographs; probably through her. I'll bet money that this isn't the first time she's done something like this. If past experience is anything to go by you won't have been the first to fall under her spell."

Doyle stopped, allowing what he had just said, to sink in. Watching Phillip, he saw how deflated he now felt as he tried to accept that what he had just been told could well be true. It was driving him crazy.

Waiting a moment, Tommy continued, "Unless we get to the bottom of this Phillip, they will not leave you alone. And, if you pay up once, they'll keep coming back again and again, until they have bled you dry. In fact, beyond that. You could end up losing your home. Do really you want that to happen at this moment in time?"

Merton shook his head, saddened by the turn of events and surprised that Doyle had sussed out what was already in his own mind. He had already admitted to himself that if he paid up then they could come back for more. He had never felt such an absolute idiot.

Finally, he said, "Okay, Mr. Doyle. I am in your hands. What do you suggest we do next?"

With Tommy being satisfied that Merton had seen sense and had agreed to co-operate, he replied, "First thing we do is go and see my friend Inspector Pete Mackintosh. He will do his level best to keep the matter as quiet as possible."

"What about my wife?"

"What about her?" Tommy asked.

"Does she have to be involved?" questioned Merton.

Shaking his head, Tommy said, "No. I'm sure we can keep her out of this."

Satisfied that Doyle would do his best for him, Phillip Merton resigned himself to what was to happen next. Shortly afterward they left the office, making their way to see Mac.

Arriving at Mac's office, the process of taking Merton's fingerprints was quickly done. Mac kept the note, sending it for forensic testing. He also kept the pictures, locking them away securely in his special safe; promising to return them to Mr. Merton to be destroyed once the matter was complete.

In the meantime, Tommy instructed Merton not to communicate with Annabel. If she did contact him, he was to arrange to meet, but Tommy would go in his place as he wanted to see what she looked like. Afterward, when she contacted Merton to complain about him not turning up, he was to say his wife was bad and she couldn't be left. After that, he was to make any excuse he could, not to meet with her at all. Merton was also to contact Tommy the moment he received an envelope that looked suspicious, which the man faithfully promised to do. Whether Mr. Merton went home feeling any relief Tommy did not know but hoped he had got some relief.

Much later, when Mac met up with Tommy, he had some interesting information to divulge. It appeared that Mr. Merton was not the first person to be caught in the blackmail trap. It appeared that a young woman called Sonia had been reported trying to do something similar last year. Unfortunately, the person concerned wouldn't co-operate with the police and had later confessed everything to his wife. They had moved out of town shortly afterward. The cases seemed very similar in both formats, and by the fact that Sonia and Annabel were described as looking the same.

* * * *

Not hearing anything from Merton for over three days Tommy wondered if the man had succumbed and paid the blackmail money. He was therefore surprised when, the following morning, a knock at the office door announced the gentleman's arrival. Entering the room, Merton said, "I don't think you expected me to return, did you, Mr. Doyle?"

Grinning, Tommy said, "If I am truthful, Phillip, then the answer has to be no. I didn't. I presume you've received another envelope."

Nodding, Merton quickly handed a large manila envelope over to Tommy, who made sure he handled it by the corner only. Laying it down on the desk he opened a Drawer; taking out a pair of forensic gloves, some tweezers, and a new plastic folder. Carefully slitting the envelope open, he used the tweezers to gently remove the note inside. The message was like the first one; made up by using cuttings from newspapers and magazines. It read: Put £20K in a plain bag. Leave in the locker at LA railway station.

Tipping the envelope upside down a locker key fell onto the desk. Merton reached out to pick it up but Tommy stopped him. Using the point of the paper knife he picked the key up to examine it. It had the number 321 embossed on the sides, and the words LA Station.

Picking up the phone Tommy rang Mac, telling him, "Hi Mac. I have Mr. Merton here. He's received an envelope; contains a note like last time and a key for a locker at LA Station. Do you want me to bring them in?"

Tommy listened to what Mac had to say, acknowledged that they would be at the precinct within the next half hour, then hung up the phone. Carefully he gathered the items together, placing them in a clean plastic bag. Shortly afterward they left the office.

Sitting in the precinct, the pair waited for Mac to return from forensics. Merton was lost in his own thoughts. He felt a real idiot for getting himself into this mess in the first place. The only consolation for him was that Doyle was being considerate in the way he was handling the matter. He hadn't shown any disgust at his indiscretion; he presumed Doyle was used to such things happening.

"Okay guys," Mac announced, entering his office. "Preliminary tests seem to show it's the same person sending the notes. Whoever it is, he's an idiot. He's so cocky about what he's doing that he hasn't even bothered to use gloves when making the note up."

Both Doyle and Merton looked up in surprise. "So, what do we do next Inspector," asked Merton.

"Well, I presume, Mr. Merton, that you don't have the money to pay these guys so we need to set up a sting. Are you able to co-operate with us on this?" asked Mac.

"If I don't have the money, I don't see how I can."

"Oh, don't worry about the money we can sort that out," responded Mac.

"Well, in that case, I am in your hands, Inspector. Just tell me what I have to do," Merton replied.

Over the next hour, plans were put in place for a sting. The Drop was to take place in three days. Mac would use Tommy as the go-between, as well as asking him to keep an eye on Mr. Merton, who had returned home to look after his sick wife.

Tommy returned to his office but not before going to the railway station to suss out the layout of the place. That evening, when Mac called to see him, they went over the plans made earlier in the day, along with a few extra's they hadn't told Mr. Merton about.

* * * *

Three days later Mr. Merton arrived at Tommy's office.

He was nervous about the forthcoming event, as well as being worried about his wife. She had been admitted to the hospital during the night. He'd had very little sleep and looked tired.

Mac arrived half an hour later with the money; or we should say, 'funny money.' It was part of a batch of counterfeit dollars they had recovered from another sting last year. The outer dollars were genuine but the rest were false. A glance would fool anyone who wasn't an expert. All were marked as well.

At the given time, the three men left Doyle's office. Merton and Tommy went direct to the station, while Mac made his own way there via a different route. He needed to check in with his men to ensure they were in place and ready.

Approaching the station Tommy instructed Merton on what he was to do. "Okay Phillip," he said. "You go in, find the locker, open the door and drop the money in. Lock the door and leave. Go straight home; do not hesitate, and do not look back."

Mr. Merton nodded his agreement. As they neared the station, Tommy whispered, "Right off you go. Remember, do as I told you, and don't look at me. Walk away. Ignore me. Do not, under any circumstances, acknowledge me," and on that note Tommy turned away, entering the station by a different door.

Despite taking a sneaky look around Merton couldn't see Mac anywhere. Following the instructions, he found the lockers. Opening the door to box 321 he quickly pushed the bag inside, locked the door, had a sneaky look around, then turning, left the station. As he left, he caught sight of Tommy standing, reading a paper but ignored him. Tommy, seeing Merton, acted as if he didn't exist; the sign of a good undercover cop.

The wait for someone to visit the locker would last about three hours. Whoever the blackmailer was, he or she was being very careful; waiting until they were sure the coast was clear.

Tommy acted the impatient husband; choosing a train that was delayed as cover for him being in the station so long. Every so often, he would look at the notice board or go to the information desk, as if chasing information.

Mac sat in the coffee bar within sight of the lockers but hiding behind a newspaper. One of the police officers was acting as a cleaner, sweeping the floor and tidying up the seats close to the lockers. A couple of other officers were moving in and out of the station; often disappearing into the toilets so they could change coats and hats etc.

After a long wait, a young woman finally approached the lockers. Carefully she looked around for anything suspicious. Once she was sure the coast was clear she put the key in locker 321 and grabbed the bag. The officer, acting as the cleaner, along with Tommy moved in fast, with Mac and the other guys following.

"Annabel, I presume?" stated Tommy smilingly as he blocked the young woman's path.

Hesitating she tried to go around him but the other officers, having closed in, had her surrounded. She had nowhere to run.

"I don't believe this belongs to you, does it?" said Tommy placing his hand on the bag and gripping it fast.

Trying to pull the bag away, Annabel looked around for a means of escape before saying, "I think you are mistaken. My name is not Annabel and this bag is mine. I do have the locker key," and she flashed the key at him.

Mac stepped forward, showing his ID card, he asked, "Well then, you won't mind telling us what's inside the bag, will you?"

It was obvious the young woman was going to try and bluff it out, responding with, "It's… it's just some old papers, that's all," and she tried to wrap her arms around the bag.

Tommy waited a moment, then with a quick tug, he pulled the bag from her arms; surprising her with his quick action. Realising the game might be up Annabel slipped around the officers and made a dash for the exit. She didn't get far, coming up short against a group of people who blocked her way, preventing her from leaving.

Catching up with her, Mac quickly slipped the handcuffs around her wrists and proceeded to tell her she was under arrest. Reading her the Miranda Rights he allowed the other two officers to escort her outside to a waiting police car.

"Slippy little thing," announced Tommy as he approached Mac, handing him the bag of money.

"Sure is," replied Mac. "Are you coming down to the station?" Nodding, Tommy got in Mac's car and they made their way to the precinct.

After the young woman had been fingerprinted, Mac interviewed her; Doyle watched and listened from the next room through the two-way mirror. It took Mac some time to break through the young woman's defences. It was obvious that even at so young an age, she was an old hand at being interviewed, quickly demanding a lawyer.

Whilst they waited Doyle rang Mr. Merton, telling him what had happened and asking him to come to the precinct to identify the young woman. He arrived an hour later looking extremely depressed.

Doyle asked, "Are you okay, Phillip."

Merton swallowed hard before looking at Tommy, who noted a small tear in the corner of his eye. Taking a deep breath he swallowed, before replying, "My wife passed away two hours ago. That's why it took me so long to get here. She never came out of the coma from last night. But I'll be okay."

Having heard similar words many times in the past, Doyle was adept at saying the right thing. "I'm very sorry Phillip. Would you prefer to leave it for today and come back tomorrow? It's just that we've arrested a young woman and we wondered if she was Annabel."

Merton's head went up at the sound of Annabel's name. Doyle wondered if he was going to have second thoughts about her so decided to let him see, and listen, to what she was saying. Taking Mr. Merton through to the room next to the interview room, he turned the speaker up so he could hear what was being said.

Mac was speaking, "Is Annabel your real name, or is it Sonia Dobson as it shows here in your record?"

The young woman listened to what the lawyer had to say before replying, "No comment."

Mac sighed, continuing, "To be honest, Sonia, I don't need you to confirm your name as your fingerprints match those of Sonia Dobson. It's not worth your effort wasting my time with all this no comment crap."

"Well, if you have the information, why are you asking me," sniggered Sonia.

"Tell me about your relationship with Mr. Phillip Merton; and the blackmail."

After listening to her lawyer, Sonia argued the point with him, finally responding with, "What do you want to know?"

"What made you take up with Mr. Merton?" asked Mac.

"He was okay. He was lonely and had money. And he showed me a good time," she responded.

"Was it your idea to blackmail him or someone else's" asked Mac?

"I don't know what you mean. Okay, so I went out with the old guy and maybe I used him. God knows he was desperate, what with that wife of his, but that's all it was, just a bit of fun, whilst it lasted. Besides, he spent money showing me a good time," and she laughed.

In the other room, Tommy watched Merton's face. It had finally begun to dawn on him what a user Annabel was. Tommy hoped that anger would take over and he would admit who she was.

Realising he was being watched Phillip turned towards Tommy, saying, "I've been a fool, haven't I? A stupid, dull old fool. Here was I, thinking she cared about me, and all the while she was using me; taking what she could. That's Annabel, or Sonia, or whatever her name is but yes that is her," and he paused, sighing sadly. "Can I go home now, Mr. Doyle?"

Nodding his head in agreement Tommy had a young officer show him out, telling him he would be in touch shortly. He felt sorry for the man. He'd just lost his wife, and now he had lost something he thought was real.

After Merton had left Tommy went back to listening to Mac interviewing the young woman. When he read out the names of several other people who had been blackmailed, telling her they were prepared to bring charges against her for these as well, she finally cracked, confessing that it hadn't been her idea to blackmail anybody.

What she said next, almost but not quite, shocked Mac and Tommy.

"It was my husband, Caleb. He planned it all," and she proceeded to tell the whole story.

Two hours later, Caleb Dobson was found, arrested, and charged with as much as Mac could throw at him. Tommy returned to his office, pleased at the final outcome.

* * * *

The following day Mr. Merton arrived at Tommy's office. He seemed more in control of his emotions as he sat, and listened, to the whole sorry affair of Annabel. Once Tommy had finished telling him the details Merton handed over a cheque to cover what he owed.

As he left, he said, "I want to thank you, Mr. Doyle. At least my wife died without knowing anything of my disgraceful behaviour. I have learnt a valuable lesson in life. Thank you."

Tommy shook his hand, responding with, "No problem Phillip. I am just glad that it was all sorted for you. Remember, we men can sometimes be victims of our own egos. Who wouldn't have their head turned when a pretty girl shows interest in them; especially at a time when we are vulnerable? You take care, Phillip."

After he had gone Tommy thought about the case. How would he react if a pretty young woman showed interest in him? Would he fall under her spell? No, he wouldn't.

But then again, maybe he would; after all, he was only human.

A GOOD CITIZEN

Locking the apartment door Doyle made his way down the stairs. As he passed his office door, he heard the telephone start to ring. Should he answer it or ignore it?

'Hell,' he thought. Unlocking the door, he crossed to the desk and picked the phone up grumbling into it, "Yea; who's this?"

"My, my, my! Aren't we grumpy this morning? Got out of the wrong side of the bed, Tommy?" laughed a familiar voice.

Laughing in response, Tommy said, "Morning, Mac. Ran out of milk so no breakfast. What you want?"

"How's about you pick up a coffee for both of us, then head on down to pier 6; we got a floater which might interest you? Oh! And Tommy... bring some donuts with you. I haven't had breakfast either," responded Mac laughingly.

"Sure," said Tommy, before hanging up. It seemed strange that Mac (Inspector Pete Mackintosh) would bring him in on a case so early; it sounded mysterious.

Half an hour later, Doyle arrived at pier six carrying two polystyrene cups of coffee, and a bag of fresh donuts. As he approached the cordoned-off area a young police officer stepped forward to stop him.

"Mackintosh is expecting me," Tommy growled. "Names Doyle."

The young officer hesitated, not sure whether to let him pass or not. Suddenly a voice boomed out, "Hey, Tommy, I hope that coffee is hot. Let him through, Preston."

It was Mac.

The young officer raised the tape, allowing Doyle to duck underneath. He passed a cup of strong black coffee to the Inspector, followed by a bag of warm donuts.

Mac looked inside the bag, smelling the freshness of the contents. "Thanks. Follow me."

Doyle trailed after Mac to an area under the bridge which crossed over the river. As they approached, he could see other officers searching the area. Kneeling on the floor was the forensic doctor who was examining what appeared to be a woman's body.

Just then someone shouted. Everyone turned towards the water's edge as another young officer yelled out, "We've got another one."

Two or three officers went forward to assist in lifting the second body from the water.

Doyle, sipping his coffee, slowly followed Mac. He needed it this morning; one body was bad, two worse. Looking over the shoulder of the young officer, Doyle noted a man's body had been lifted out of the dirty water. Strangely the guy was Dressed in a tuxedo. This was no ordinary bum who'd gotten Drunk and fallen over the edge of the pier.

Doctor Martin came over and quickly examined the second body.

"Well, Doc," asked Mac, "what do you think?"

Standing, the Doctor reported. "On preliminary inspection, there doesn't appear to be any wounds; no excessive blood. There does appear to have been a blow to the back of the head; could be from the fall. I'll know more when I get them both back to the morgue. Am I clear to remove the bodies, Mac?"

"Yea, go ahead, Doc. Let me know when you have some results," he replied before turning away to give instructions to the crew.

"Well, hello stranger," said the Doc. "And how are you, Tommy?"

Doyle hesitated before replying. "Err… not bad, Doctor Martin. And you, how are you?"

"Why so formal, Tommy? Has it been that long you've forgotten my name?" she teasingly questioned him.

Doyle was not one to blush, but Veronica Martin, ME, could sure bring him pretty close to doing so. He swallowed before replying, "Didn't think it correct whilst you're on the job, Veronica. So, how you doing; you married that young man of yours yet?"

Veronica laughed lightly. "Oh, Tommy, you are so out of date. We split up about a year ago. At the moment, I'm available if you're interested?" and she laughed as she walked away. Doyle watched her thoughtfully.

"Watch yourself, Tommy lad; that's one hell of a lady," said Mac. "Perhaps she's still got the hots for you!" and he laughed out loud at his joke, before walking off to speak to his officers.

'Hell," thought Tommy, "she's still got it; whatever 'It' is."

If he were honest, Tommy would have to admit that he found Veronica Martin one hell of a woman. He always had, but at the time they worked together she had been involved with a young, good-looking, rich guy, so he had kept his distance.

They'd worked closely on quite a few homicides during his time on the force, always getting on well together. Doyle had been divorced ten years when Veronica came on the scene. He would have willingly dated her; had she been interested. But that was back then.

'Better forget it," he thought.

Going over to speak to Mac, he enquired, "So, why are we meeting here. What's so special about these two floaters?"

"Come on back to the precinct and I'll explain more," replied Mac.

About an hour later Doyle sat drinking coffee in Mac's office, listening to the details of the dead bodies. It turned out the man was The Honourable James Brigham. He was British Aristocracy; son of a wealthy titled gentleman who was big in finance. Brigham had been found wearing a tuxedo, black shoes, and a dicky bow; the complete outfit for a man attending a 'formal' do. His watch appeared to be missing, but his wallet had been found inside his back pocket, complete with a driving licence, credit cards, and money.

The woman had likewise been dressed formally, in an expensive evening gown. She had still been wearing her jewellery; a ruby necklace with a bracelet to match, a diamond-studded watch, and diamond earrings, but no shoes.

Doyle listened, thinking about the information, before commenting. "Seems like a couple of Drunks on a yacht falling overboard. Or one of them fell over, and the other one dived into the rescue. No obvious assault injuries that the Doc could see, so no murder. Where's the problem, Mac?"

"The woman has been named as Jacqueline Heinrichman," replied Mac. "She's the daughter of a very wealthy German industrialist. Brigham is the son of a financier, and British to boot. The Chief is not happy that two important, very wealthy people, died on the same night in the same way."

Doyle shrugged his shoulders. "So, why call me? What aren't you telling me, Mac?"

Mac swallowed, taking his time before answering. "It seems that Mr. Heinrichman, the girl's father, has requested that a certain Detective Doyle be put on the case."

"What," Doyle almost shouted. "Did you tell him I don't work here anymore?"

"Yea, of course, I did. However, the gentleman went straight upstairs; direct to the Commissioner and he has demanded that you personally handle the investigation."

Knowing Doyle would not be pleased with this answer, Mac waited for the explosion. He knew that Tommy and the Commissioner did not get on. In fact, they disliked each other a great deal so he hadn't been sure how Doyle would react to the request.

In order to give his pal time to cool down, he continued. "It appears that it's Mrs. Heinrichman who knows you, and it is she who has recommended you to her husband. And apparently, what that lady wants, that lady gets. So, what do you say?"

Doyle looked at Mac, distaste pulsating through him at the very idea of agreeing to do anything the Commissioner wanted. Finally, he answered, "I don't know any Mrs. Heinrich-whatever her name is; never heard of her."

"Well, she knows you and knows you well. The Commissioner has asked me... no, he's actually ordered me, to take you back into the office. You will be paid your usual fee and, if the matter can be resolved quickly and efficiently, you'll get a bonus. As for someone to work with, that's going to be me. I managed to talk the Commissioner, and the Chief, into putting me in charge of the case. So, what do you say, Tommy lad, will you do it?"

Doyle thought long and hard before responding. "Well, I suppose. But if it was anybody else other than you the answer would be a flat no; whether the dame knows me or not. So, what's next?"

Mac heaved a big sigh, relief crossing his face which Doyle noticed. He liked Mac; they'd been good mates throughout his time on the force; at least he could trust him. As for the money and the bonus, well it all helps he supposed. Not that he needed the extra cash but it meant he need not work if didn't feel like it.

Knowing what Doyle's reaction could have been, Mac was exceedingly relieved by him agreeing to work with him. He liked Tommy, always had. Besides, he owed the guy his life – literally.

It was Doyle who had once saved him from being shot by a two-bit punk who thought he could rob a convenience store. The guy had cornered Mac in an alleyway after he had chased him for two blocks. The punk had been a bit of a nutter, thinking the idea of killing a cop would be fun.

Just as he was about to pull the trigger, Doyle had appeared from around the corner and shot the gun out of the perp's hand. Mac had never felt such relief in the whole of his life; he owed Tommy for that one, and he knew it.

"Okay," announced Mac. "Mr. Heinrichman has requested a meeting at three o'clock this afternoon in his suite at the Palace Lake hotel. Before we go, let's get a bite to eat, and see if the Doc has any further results for us." Having agreed on their plan of action the pair left the precinct.

Later, at the morgue, Doyle and Mac stood waiting to hear what the Doctor had to tell them if anything at all. "You're eager, Mac. What's so special about these two? I've even had the Chief on at me about getting the autopsy done, pretty damn quick. I've never known him to be so interested in a body before."

Mac looked at Veronica. "Important people, Doc. We need the results a.s.a.p."

Veronica nodded her head, starting the short report on what she had found out so far. "Both had drowned, neither appearing to have suffered any wounds, yet both had a swelling on the back of their heads. Probably from falling overboard, although it could have been from a blow by a blunt instrument. Until I dig further, I can't confirm it," she informed them. She always spoke in her official voice when giving a report, not the gentle teasing one she had used earlier.

Tommy stood to one side, so he could silently watch her. The years had been good to the Doc. She was as attractive now as she had been the last time, he had seen her, which was nearly four years ago. Suddenly, he realised she was speaking to him. "Sorry, Doc, you were saying," he asked.

"I wondered why you were here, that was all," she replied questioningly.

Doyle looked at Mac who took the lead, responding, "Special assignment, Doc. He's working alongside me on this one; orders from upstairs."
The Doctor looked surprised but knew better than to ask any further. If Mac wanted to tell her more then he would, if not she would learn no more.

With nothing else to report the pair left the Doctor with her thoughts. But if Doyle could have read her mind, he might have been pleasantly surprised by them.

It was ten minutes to three when Mac and Doyle walked into the Palace Lake Hotel, an old established place built in the golden age of the nineteen-thirties. Over the years it had lost its lustre, but two years ago a hotel chain had purchased it, spending an absorbent amount of money renovating it, and bringing it back up to five-star standards. Both Doyle and Mac were impressed.

The Bell Boy escorted the pair upstairs to the Heinrichman's suite. Money talked and privacy was obviously honoured; not just anyone got into the hallowed realms of the upper floors. Arriving at the suite (all suites being named after old Movie Stars, this one after Sir Lawrence Olivier) the bell boy rang the doorbell; waiting to ensure that the gentlemen were indeed expected. The door was opened by the butler. Having confirmed the two were indeed welcome the bell boy left.

"Come in gentlemen," requested the Butler. "Mr. Heinrichman will be with you shortly. Can I get you any refreshments?"

Both Doyle and Mac declined, neither felt inclined to sit down as the quality of the place intimidated even them. Nothing was said, but a knowing look passed between the pair. Mac chose to inspect a painting on the wall, whilst Tommy stood and stared out of the large picture windows from which he could see most of the city.

"Tommy Doyle; is that really you?" asked a soft, refined voice.

Shocked, Doyle recalled the last time he had heard that voice. Turning slowly around, he stood staring at the woman who was waiting for his response. A good-looking woman he never forgot, and he had certainly never forgotten this one. Swallowing hard he slowly walked towards her.

Out of the corner of his eye, he could see Mac looking, questioningly, wondering how Tommy knew this gorgeous-looking woman.

"Surely you haven't forgotten me, Tommy?" asked the woman before stepping towards Mac and introducing herself, "Good afternoon, Inspector Mackintosh, I'm Kristy Heinrichman, please sit down."

The introduction had given Tommy the chance he needed to gather his thoughts and his memories.

Approaching the woman, he held out his hand to shake hers, saying, "Kristy, what a pleasant surprise to see you."

She laughed at him, but instead of shaking his hand, she leant forward to kiss him on the cheek, whispering, "What a delight to see you again, Tommy," before stepping away and asking him to sit down.

"My husband will be joining us shortly. It takes him a little longer to get ready these days but he's eager to meet you Tommy; both of you," and she smiled at Mac. As she did so it seemed as if the sun had suddenly begun to shine. Her smile lighting up her face, and the room.

Just then the Butler arrived with a tea trolley and proceeded to serve them. Kristy announced, "I am afraid I take tea these days, so I hope you will join me?"

Both men accepted a delicate cup and saucer which they immediately placed down on the small table next to where they were sat.

The interlude had given Tommy a chance to gather his wits, and Mac a chance to examine the woman more closely. She looked to be aged about thirty, but in reality, was nearer forty. Her figure was slim and her dress elegant. She wore matching shoes and jewellery that was obviously quite expensive.

'A woman of the world,' thought Mac. 'How the hell does Tommy know her?'

At last, Doyle managed to speak, asking, "Well, Kristy, this is a surprise; so, how are you doing, obviously well."

Kristy turned to look at him, a smile in her eyes, as she responded with, "Yes, I am, and it's all thanks to you."

Both Mac and Doyle were surprised by the comment. Doyle asked, "And what makes you think that, Kristy?"

"Oh, come on, Tommy. If it hadn't been for you putting me on the straight and narrow, I would never have moved back home, never have met Frederick, nor be as happy as I am now."

Turning towards Mac she began explaining how some years ago she had got caught up with the wrong crowd. That's when she had met Doyle. He had come across her, and seeing something good in her, had given her a strong talking to. Then he had bought her a one-way train ticket and sent her home.

Going back had changed her life for the better. She had applied for a job at the Heinrichman country home. Meeting Frederick there, she had got to know him well, eventually becoming a companion to him. His family, a daughter, and a son had been happy with the arrangement. Both were wrapped up with their own lives, spending little, or no time with their father.

As Frederick had become incapacitated, being confined to a wheelchair, the couple had been drawn closer together. Love had finally blossomed, and they had married some seven years ago. Kristy couldn't have children of her own, which is probably why Frederick's children had approved of the marriage.

Also, knowing their Father's finances had been put in order before their marriage, meant they wouldn't lose their inheritance, so they were quite happy for Kristy to have her share, once Frederick passed away. Both were already highly successful in their own right, so the small annual annuity she would get, was of little importance to them.

Mac surprised by the confession, and knowing none of this, looked at Tommy, an unasked question on his face. Doyle smiled at the memory, remembering what a comical young woman she had been; a girl really, and a very frightened one at that.

Finally, Tommy said, "You've done well, Kristy and you look very happy."

"Oh, I am," she replied with a smile, "Very happy. I want to thank you, Tommy, for doing what you did. That's why I suggested you handle the case. I didn't realise you didn't work for the police anymore."

"Yea," he smiled in return. "I resigned over three years ago. I'm a PI now, but I work closely with Mac, my ex-partner. He's in charge; I just give help when needed."

At that moment, a door opened and a tall, gaunt-looking man entered; he was pushing a wheelchair in which an older man sat, wrapped in a blanket. Wheeling the chair across the room he placed it next to Kristy. Once the chair was settled, she reached out, taking hold of the man's hand, saying, "Frederick, darling, this is Inspector Mackintosh. And, this is Tommy Doyle, the man I told you about."

Both Doyle and Mac rose from their seats, approaching Heinrichman to shake his hand which proved to be firm. As he took hold of Doyle's hand, he looked into his eyes. "Mr. Doyle, I want to thank you for all you did for my Kristy. Without your assistance, I would not be the happiest of men; thank you."

Doyle felt embarrassed at the compliment, trying to shrug it off, but inside he felt satisfaction at what he had achieved. Sitting back down, he replied, "It was nothing, Sir. I am just glad to see Kristy, Mrs. Heinrichman, looking so happy and well."

Heinrichman smiled warmly, replying, "Please, Mr. Doyle, call me Frederick, and of course, Kristy. And may I call you, Tommy? And you, of course, Inspector, how should we refer to yourself?"

"Mac, Sir, err Frederick. I'd be honoured to address you both so, but not when the Commissioner or the Chief is around," and Mac laughed, lightening the atmosphere in the room.

For the next hour, Doyle and Mac spent their time learning as much as they could about Jacqueline Heinrichman. Frederick was very open about his daughter and her relationship with James Brigham. What he couldn't work out was why someone would want to kill either of them. Both were wealthy, so kidnapping would have been the better option if money was the goal. But murder? For Frederick believed it was murder.

By the time Doyle and Mac left they were no nearer in solving, or in finding a reason for the deaths. They now had some idea of the people the couple knew, Kristy telling them to contact her if they needed any more information or introductions to people.

Outside, Mac asked, "So what do you think, Tommy?"

"Right now, I'm not sure. Think I'll go back to the office and do some research on the internet, what about you?"

"The same thing; meet you later at O'Malley's," he replied. Agreeing, the two parted, after settling on a time to meet later that evening.

Back in his office, Tommy sat for a while mulling over the day's events, before switching on his computer. He was pleased about Kristy. She'd had a bad time in the city; having met the wrong guy she'd become pregnant. The man had beaten her up and she'd lost the baby. The lucky thing was, she had got out before getting caught up in drugs, or anything worse. He was glad she had Frederick. The man obviously loved her and was taking good care of her.

Putting Kristy out of his mind, Doyle settled down to search the net for information on both victims. Perhaps he could turn up something of interest about them. Two hours later he switched the computer off. He had searched for some time, coming up with snippets of information that might prove to be of use. He would talk things over with Mac when they met later; but for now, he was going to get showered and changed.

* * * *

The investigation didn't go far for the next couple of days. Mac and Doyle agreed on a list of names of people to interview. These were people who had been at the party the two victims had attended.

As Mac entered his office the following morning he was surprised to discover the Commissioner sat at his desk reading his files.

"Good morning, Commissioner," Mac announced his presence.

The Commissioner jumped up, a guilty look on his face. He quickly closed the file he had been reading. "Morning, Mackintosh. I was wondering when you were going to close this drowning case.

Should be a simple accident; both get drunk, fall overboard and drown. Why is it going on so long?"

Mac looked at the Commissioner questioningly. It seemed very strange for the man to be pushing to close a case so quickly.

'What the hell is going on,' thought Mac. Clearing his throat, he replied, "Should be able to call it once the last of the interviews are done. A couple of people we missed have been out of town, but are due back today, so we'll catch up with them later. Besides, Commissioner, you're always drumming it into us that we should dot every 'i' and cross every 't'. We don't want to miss anything, do we?"

Reluctantly the Commissioner agreed, and as he left the office, he said, "Yes, well, get on with it."

Mac sat down, thinking over what had just happened. It was very strange that the man would come into his office, pushing him hard on this one case.

Opening the file, he read the contents again; trying to decide what they might have missed. Something didn't seem, right? Maybe Tommy could bring another perspective to the situation. Picking up the Brigham and Heinrichman files, Mac left the precinct, heading for Doyle's office.

The brownstone always looked as if it was run down; at least on the outside. Doyle kept it that way for a reason. It deterred burglars. The inside, however, was completely different; very secure and alarmed to the roof. Pressing the intercom button, Mac announced himself into the speaker.

The outer door lock clicked as he pushed it open. Passing into the small entrance, the outer door locked behind him before the inner door, into the hallway, clicked open. Double security, for when Doyle was upstairs. There were security cameras discreetly installed, and Mac knew that Doyle had TV screens showing who was entering the building.

Mounting the stairs Mac found the door to Doyle's office open. As he entered, the smell of coffee assailed his nostrils. Tommy was sat at his desk finishing a phone call. He waved towards the coffee machine indicating Mac should help himself to a cup. This he did, before sitting in the chair on the opposite side of the desk.

Finishing his call, Tommy replaced the receiver and looked at Mac. He realised the man was worried. "Morning, Mac. What's up?"

Swallowing, Mac told him about the Commissioner's visit. He passed the two files he had brought with him across the desk for Doyle to look at.

"We must be missing something," he said. "Either that or I must be getting old cause I sure as hell don't know what it is."

Doyle opened the files to read them; he sat thinking, all the while doodling on the pad in front of him. Finally, he said, "Maybe we need to start from scratch. Look at it from a different angle."

Mac nodded. Sighing, he replied, "Okay. What do you suggest we do?"

"Right," stated Tommy, "Let's go back to basics," and they spent the next hour reviewing the whole case.

Finally, both guys sat back, satisfied with the results of their brainstorming session.

"Okay," said Tommy, "what we've done is get bogged down without looking at the case properly. We've accepted that it was a drunk drowning, without questioning the evidence. The first thing we need to do is double-check with the ME; make sure she's done all the right tests; toxicology, alcohol levels, etc. Then, we need to re-check the people who were present on the yacht at the time. Make sure we haven't missed anyone," and he started to look through the files.

"Mac, don't you have a copy of the guest list?" he asked.

Looking up in surprise, Mac replied, "Yea, it's in the file."

"No, it isn't, so maybe that's where we should start," replied Doyle. "Back to basics; a full investigation as if we'd never been approached by Heinrichman."

The next couple of hours were spent in concentrated work. Mac contacted the Sheik who had hosted the part and had a fresh copy of the guest list sent to Tommy's email. While they waited for the list to come through Tommy spoke to the ME, getting her to email a new copy of the autopsy direct to him.

The email pinged and Mac printed off the sheet containing the guest list. He was reading the list when he let out a whistle, then he swore loudly.

Tommy, looking up from his computer asked, "What's the matter?"

Mac passed the list to him before responding, "This isn't the same list I received. The one I had was doctored. Certain people were omitted from my copy. Now why is that, I wonder. And, more importantly, who managed to delete them?

Tommy pressed print on the computer to print off the report sent by the ME, before taking the list proffered to him. As he read it, he whistled too. Then looking at Mac, he said, "What the hell has been happening here, Mac. This isn't the list you showed me the other day. There are some very interesting names on it which weren't there before. Are you sure this is correct?"

Mac nodded, before going to the printer to collect the printed report. Once again, he whistled and swore loudly. Sitting at the desk he opened the file, taking out the copy of the ME's report he had originally received. He compared the two.

Doyle asked, "So, what's wrong with the ME's document?"

"It's also been doctored," responded Mac. "Someone amended the details before I got a copy." And he passed across the report.

Reading it, Tommy too was surprised at the differences, asking, "When you got the original document who delivered it?"

Thinking for a moment, Mac said, "I don't know. They were sat on my desk when I got to the office. Ring the Doc and see when she delivered it, will you please. I want to recheck the list against the interviews already done."

Picking up the phone, Tommy dialled the number for the morgue. Ten minutes later he came off the line. Mac looked questioningly, wanting to know what the Doc had said.

"According to Veronica, the report was collected by the Commissioner's Secretary. She said she did think it was unusual but with the Commissioner having been pressing her for a quick result, due to the victim's father being in communiqué with him, she just accepted the urgency without question. She wanted to know if there was a problem with it. I told her no. Told her you'd spilled coffee on the file. Okay."

Mac nodded his head in agreement, before going back to the guest list. "Did you notice who was on the list?" asked Mac, "Our old friend, Jo-Jo Grimondi."

Tommy nodded. "Well, well well! Our favourite Italian mobster. And, Penelope Davis; number one call girl. I think we need to pay a couple of visits, don't you?"

Mac agreed, and within fifteen minutes the pair were on their way but not before Tommy had locked the two files away in a secret compartment, only he and Mac knew the location off. After all, you never knew that even with his additional security someone could still break-in and he was having none of that.

Their first port of call was to Grimondi's place – The Green Hawk; a nightclub, known as the place to go when looking for bad guys. Entering, a couple of heavy guys stood up to intercept them. Tommy spoke, "We're looking for Jo-Jo."

"He's not here," said one of the guys gruffly, "So get lost."

Doyle didn't budge. Staring the guy down, he was working out where to hit him the hardest, in order to stop him in his tracks. These types often thought they were tough but hit them in the right place and they went down like a ton of bricks. The guy stared at Doyle who stared right back, just as menacingly. The atmosphere was electric.

"Well, well, well," announced a voice from the back of the room. "If it isn't my favourite ex-cop, Tommy Doyle. Oh, and Inspector Mac. Back off Gino, these are friends. Come in gentlemen."

Walking to the back of the room to sit at a table, Tommy studied Jo-Jo. It had been a while since he had last set eyes on the young mobster. 'Looks like he was going to fat a little,' he thought.

Sitting down Tommy and Mac accepted the coffee, although neither touched the drink. You never knew when someone might try to slip you a 'mickey.'

"So, to what do I owe this honour," asked Jo-Jo.

Mac pulled out the two photos of the drowned victims, passing them across to Jo-Jo. He took them, and studied them, before passing them back, saying, "They look dead."

"They are," replied Tommy. "And they were on the same yacht as you when it happened. Funny coincidence that Jo-Jo, don't you think!"

Grimondi looked at Tommy, surprise for a moment written on his face. "Don't know what ya' referring to," he replied.

"Now, that's very strange," interrupted Mac. "Because, according to the list I received from the Sheik, there just happens to be a Mr. J Grimondi listed as a guest. Considering you're the only J Grimondi in town, I think we can safely presume it's you."

"Yea so quit messing us about, and answer the bloody question," Tommy growled at him.

"Okay, okay, guys, take it easy. Yea, I was at the party. The Sheik's an okay kind of guy," responded Jo-Jo.

"Sure, so I'll ask you again, did you see either of these two," asked Mac.

Swallowing hard Jo-Jo began telling Tommy and Mac about the evening of the party. Yea, he'd seen the woman, and probably the man, but only in passing. Maybe they would do better talking to Penny Davis. She might be able to tell them more.

Realising that they would get no more from Jo-Jo, the pair bade him goodbye and left the club.

Their next stop was the Blue Parrot Bar and Penelope Davis. Penny was the highest-paid call girl in town. She'd been in the business for twenty-odd years, buying the Blue Parrot about five years ago. She ran a clean joint and there had been very little trouble reported since.

The place was half empty when Tommy and Mac arrived, but they spotted Penny sat at the back of the room. Spying the pair Penny left the booth she was sat in and walked over to the bar where they stood waiting.

Penny was well over forty but looked a good ten years younger, with the figure and stature to go with it.

'Still one hell of a looker,' thought Mac.

"Why, hello boys, long time no see," she drawled in her deep Texan voice; the accent being as strong now as when she first arrived in town. "And to what do I owe the pleasure? Come for a little drink with an old friend?"

Mac smiling, answered, "Looking for some information, Penny. Are you free to give us ten minutes?"

Penny looked from Mac to Doyle. "Why of course; anything for the boys in blue," and she smiled before turning away, leading them to the back of the room and through a door marked private. The stairs behind the door led upstairs to her private domain. She liked living over the place; saying it was easier to keep an eye on things if she was on the spot.

Upstairs the 'boys' took a seat each, while Penny sat in the chair behind her desk. "Okay, Mac, what do you want to know," she asked.

Mac explained about the yacht and the party. At the mention that the drowning was probably a murder, Penny went white. "Why come to me," she asked shakily.

"Because you were there, and Jo-Jo says you might just have seen something important," replied Doyle.

Penny didn't respond. Doyle could see she was afraid of something but he was at a loss to understand what, why or who. Leaning forward he looked into her eyes, asking, "What are you afraid of Penny, or should I say, who are you afraid of?"

Penny took a moment to gather her thoughts, answering, "Afraid, who me, no way."

Mac realised that she was hiding something, so decided to put some pressure on her, "Come on, Penny, you know and I know, you're holding something back. Don't mess us around. I want to know what you heard or saw. This is a murder investigation, and I'm not going to hold any punches to get to the truth. Either you start talking, or I start acting. How about I make sure you get raided, every night, for the next three weeks. Will that help you remember?"

Tommy, surprised by Mac's reaction, felt some sympathy for Penny. He knew his pal was desperate to get to the bottom of the matter, so he really couldn't object if he used a bit of pressure to get results.

"Okay, okay, you don't have to get heavy with me. I'll tell you what I know but you'd better make sure I'm kept safe, or else," responded Penny. She then went on to explain what she had seen and heard that fateful night.

Twenty minutes later Mac and Doyle were sat downstairs discussing what to do next. The information they had just received made a big difference to the case. It also gave Mac a big headache because now he wasn't quite sure what to do. He still had to prove the case, but how?

After tossing the problem back and forth, the pair finally came up with a plan. It was risky, and it could backfire, but hopefully, the right people would pay for the crime.

With their plans in place, Tommy escorted Penny back to his place with an overnight bag. The first thing to do was to get her to make a statement and sign it. He also needed to make sure she was safe.

Back in his office, he set up the recording machine and Penny gave her statement. When she had finished, he typed it into his computer, amended any mistakes, and printed it off. Penny read through what he had typed then she signed the statement.

Tommy made four copies; one for him, one for Penny, and two for Mac. Then he showed her up to his apartment, leaving her to settle into the spare bedroom. She would be staying for a few days.

In the meantime, Mac went to see the Heinrichman's. They would also need their co-operation. Fortunately, whilst shocked at what Mac told them, they were still more than willing to help. After he left, they were the ones who set the wheels in motion.

* * * *

Three days later Doyle, Mac, and Penelope Davis arrived at the Palace Lake Hotel for lunch with Mr. & Mrs. Heinrichman in their suite. The meal was delightful and the atmosphere helped to settle Penny's nerves.

Just before two o'clock, the doorbell rang, and Heinrichman's three guests discreetly withdrew into one of the bedrooms. A minute later three new guests were shown into the lounge; Police Commissioner Wilson, the Police Chief, and the State Governor, Tom Harris. All were welcomed warmly.

Once sat, Mr. Heinrichman asked the opening question, "What was happening with the case of his daughter's death?"

The Chief told him that as far as he knew the case was practically closed and would be classed as an accidental death due to drowning, whilst intoxicated. Frederick Heinrichman, looking puzzled, told the Chief, he understood new evidence would prove otherwise.

The Commissioner jumped in, saying, "I think you must have it wrong, Frederick; there is no new evidence. I am sure Inspector Mackintosh will verify this."

"Do you think so? Mmm… that's strange because according to Inspector Mackintosh my daughter was murdered," responded Frederick. At that point, Mac and Doyle entered the lounge. Seeing them the Governor immediately stood up, making his excuses to leave.

"Oh, don't go, Governor. I'm sure you're going to find this very interesting. After all, it affects you as much as anyone," announced Tommy, crossing the room, and forcing the man to return to the seat he had just vacated.

The Chief said, "What the hell are you doing, Doyle?"

"Inviting the Governor to stay and enjoy the moment," responded Doyle, blocking the exit door.

"Doyle," yelled the Commissioner, "You get the hell out of the way. I am leaving. You are fired and are no longer needed on this case. And, as for you Mackintosh, I'm going to have your badge."

"Sit down, Wilson," announced Heinrichman severely, "You too, Governor Harris. None of you are leaving. Boris, guard the door, please." And Heinrichman's bodyguard moved to block it.

"And now, Inspector, the floor is yours," announced Heinrichman, "Go ahead."

Mac took a deep breath as he began telling the story of the night on the yacht.

"You see, gentlemen, it appears that someone has been playing games with me. And the worst is I nearly fell for it."

Taking another deep breath, he went on. "Let me explain: Firstly, someone intercepted both the report from the ME and the guest list. The strange thing is they weren't actually delivered to me direct; I just found them sat on my desk. As such, I presumed that one of the guys in the office had signed for them. This wasn't the case, so I requested copies of the original documents, and guess what I discovered?"

Mac paused, to see if anyone would answer him; no one did. "Let's take the guest list first. According to the Sheik, there were four extra people listed on the original copy: Jo-Jo Grimondi, Penelope Davis, Commissioner Wilson, and, funnily enough, you Governor Harris. Four names that had been removed from the list I received. Now why, I ask myself."

"That one's easy," interrupted Tommy. "Because someone didn't want us questioning any of those four, which makes it look very suspicious."

"Now look here, Mackintosh, I'm not putting up with any more of this. You're fired," shouted the Commissioner standing.

191

Doyle, stepping in front of the Commissioner, pushed him back into his seat, saying in a low voice, "If I were you, I would sit back down and be quiet, or, I might just have to smack you; Commissioner, or no Commissioner, I really don't care."

The man went white at the menacing sound of Doyle's voice, causing Mac to smile. Tommy had been waiting a long time to do that. He should stop him but what the hell, let him have his fun.

"Okay," continued Mac. "So, now we have all calmed down, I'll carry on. The next interception was with the ME's report. According to the one I had in the file both victims were drunk. However, when Doyle checked a second copy against the one I received, we discovered that only Brigham had any alcohol in his system."

Mac paused, allowing the information to sink in. "You see, Miss Heinrichman didn't drink. And the reason she didn't was due to the fact, that if she drank alcohol it affected her badly, giving her chronic migraines. She had recently started taking some very strong tablets to help control the problem. Her blood-alcohol level was in fact... zero."

Again, he paused to see if there was any reaction to what he was saying, then he said, "Tommy, why don't you continue telling the tale."

"Sure, why not," said Doyle, moving to stand in a place where they could watch him. "Having discovered the anomalies in the guest list we decided to interview the first two missing names; Grimondi and Penelope Davis. Grimondi couldn't tell us very much as he hadn't seen or heard anything. But Penelope, now she was a different kettle of fish. Oh yes. As it happens she told us a great deal that was very interesting." He waited to see if anyone would react before continuing.

"Well, it seems Penelope, whilst on the yacht, needed the bathroom and off she went to look for one. She was just about to leave when she heard voices. Switching the light out in the bathroom, she quietly opened the door a fraction to peek out. She saw three men arguing. Not wanting to be found she stayed silent, waiting and listening to what was being said. Unfortunately, she couldn't quite make out all the conversation. Until one of the men began yelling that he had had enough and made to leave the cabin. But just as he was about to leave one of the other men picked up a statue, and hit him over the head." Again Tommy waited, watching for any reaction.

"The third man seemed to panic, declaring the man who had been hit was dead. Then the one who had lashed out told this man to check the coast was clear. They were going to throw the victim overboard. It would be put down as an accidental drowning. The second man left the cabin returning a couple of minutes later. Quickly the pair picked up the unconscious guy, dragged him out of the cabin, and threw him overboard. As soon as they left Penny sneaked out of the cabin and went looking for Grimondi; she had come to the party with him. He arranged for them to leave the yacht immediately."

There was silence. Suddenly, Governor Harris stood up, saying, "I can't see what this has to do with me. I think I will leave now, Commissioner," and he headed for the door, only to be stopped by Boris.

"No, I think not, Governor," announced Mac, "You see, you were one of the men in the room and you, Commissioner, are the other. You two committed the murder."

"Don't be so ridiculous," shouted Commissioner Wilson. "How dare you accuse us of murder. You are going to be very sorry for this insult; taking the word of a call girl, a prostitute over us."

"Yea," replied the Governor. "Besides, you have no proof."

At this point, Mac, stepping forward, said, "Well, you see that's where you are wrong. Mr. Brigham was found without his watch; a very expensive and unique watch. His father sent me the details. There was an inscription on the backplate, in Latin. Now I understand that you like unusual items, Governor. You obviously took a fancy to it so removed it before throwing him overboard."

Mac stopped. The room was silent and tense, everyone now looked at the Governor who had turned from being purple with rage to white with fear.

Mac asked, "Would you like to know how I know all this? Well, this morning while you were in a meeting, we served a search warrant on your town flat, and guess what we found, the very watch belonging to James Brigham."

"I... I... found it on the deck of the yacht," announced the Governor, shakily appealing with his eyes for those present to believe him. "As I said, you have no proof or witnesses."

"Really," asked Mac, "Penny, can you come in here and tell us if you can identify the men who were in the cabin that night?"

Penny walked into the room and looking around she pointed to the Governor and then the Commissioner, saying, "Those are the two. I would recognise their voices anywhere. And besides, I saw them in the light from the corridor as they left the cabin."

Mac turned to the Chief, "I have to ask you this Chief, so forgive me if I'm wrong. Are you in on this cover-up, or have you been fooled the same way we have?"

The Chief smiled. "You are right to ask Mac, and I can assure you, that if I had known what was happening, I would have blown this case wide open immediately. What do you want to do now?"

"Arrest them," he replied. Turning towards the Governor and the Commissioner he read them their rights, whilst Boris let the waiting police officers outside into the room. As the pair were removed, protesting their innocence, the Chief turned to Mr. Heinrichman to apologise. Then he left, telling Mac and Tommy, he would see them back at the precinct.

Turning to face Mr. Heinrichman, Mac held out his hand. Shaking it, he thanked him for his assistance, before following the Chief out of the room.

Tommy held out his hand. Frederick taking hold shook it warmly, asking, "So, they killed both Brigham and Jacqueline then?"

Tommy looked at him. "Actually… no Frederick. They didn't kill your daughter; her death was an accident. From what we can gather, she had left the ballroom to get some fresh air. As she stood on the deck below looking at the sea, she heard a splash. She presumed Brigham had fallen overboard, so she did the only thing she could do. She yelled for help, slipped off her shoes, and dived in to save him. Unfortunately, the material of her dress soaked up that much water it became too heavy, meaning she couldn't swim properly. I am sorry to say, that she drowned trying to save Brigham's life."

"So, my daughter died for no reason," said Frederick.

"I wouldn't say 'no' reason, Frederick. Yes, it is tragic she died, but she did so doing what she thought was for the best. You have to accept, that had the circumstances been different, and had she saved Brigham, then we would have been stood here praising her for her bravery; for being a good citizen," replied Tommy.

Thinking over what Tommy had just said, sadly Frederick found he had to agree.

Saying his goodbyes, Tommy wished Frederick and Kristy all the best, then he too left the room.

It was as Doyle waited for the lift to arrive that he found Kristy had followed him out.

"Tommy, my husband has asked me to give you this," and she handed him an envelope. Then kissing him on the cheek she returned to the suite, closing the door firmly behind her.

Getting into the lift, Tommy opened the envelope, surprised by its contents. As he left the hotel, he found Mac waiting for him. "Do you want a lift, Tommy?"

Doyle looked at his friend. "No thanks, Mac. I think I'll walk."

"What you got there, Tommy," asked Mac.

Doyle showed him the cheque, causing Mac to whistle and say, "Now, that's what I call a bonus. That's a lot of money?"

"Sure is. Do you think I should take it?" asked Doyle.

"Of course, you should," responded Mac as he got into his car. "Besides, with that amount, you can afford dinner. I'll see you in O'Malley's at about eight. You're paying," and he drove away laughing.

Watching his pal leave, Doyle smiled at him, before turning to walk down the street. What a day. But how satisfying. He'd got one over on the Commissioner at last. They say all good things come to those who wait.

'I've waited long enough,' he thought as strolled along. 'That's two cases closed at last!'

ABOUT THE AUTHOR

Ann Brady is an award-winning author of historical fiction, as well as of Children's Picture Storybooks and other genres. She is also a speaker and writers mentor of many years standing.

Doyle's Casebook was one of Ann's first forays into the world of fiction writing, after spending many successful years as a non-fiction writer for an award-winning website, magazines, national newspapers, and educational tutorials.

Currently, Ann works with MentoringWriters.co.uk as their principal mentor where she assists writers of all ages worldwide to understand, learn, and discover the joys of progressing their own writing journey towards being a successful published author.

She also works with the Kids4Kids Organisation a charity she set up some twenty years ago to alongside young people, initially through the element of sport, but these days through writing. To date, Kids4Kids.org.uk has mentored several children, and publishing a few.

If you need help with your writing then you can contact Ann through any of the following websites:

www.ann-brady.co.uk

www.annbradybooks.co.uk

www.mentoringwriters.co.uk

www.kids4kids.org.uk

Ann's books can be found on Amazon, her own websites, and all good bookshops.

'ANOTHER VISIT TO'
DOYLE'S CASEBOOK

We revisit the case files of
Tommy Doyle
Private Investigator

New Book

Coming Soon